"I can't remembe

Jordan blinked. "Noth

"Not even my own name."

Biting back a curse, he shoved his fingers through his hair. Attractive and vulnerable as she was, his intention had been to walk away from this beautiful stranger. Amnesia threw an unexpected kink into his plan.

"Didn't I have a purse, a wallet, something with identification?"

"You weren't carrying anything last night." Common sense screamed to let her go, but his conscience wasn't listening. "But you did speak to my boss before you were attacked."

"Well?"

"You didn't tell her your name. You asked a question."

"Don't make me drag it out of you." Her throaty voice rose an octave. "What did I say to her?"

Jordan sank into a chair, and stared at the woman in front of him with a gut-wrenching sensation of inevitability.

"You asked her where to find *me*. You needed professional protection."

Dear Reader,

You've told us that you love amnesia stories—and in response we've created a program just for these incredibly romantic, emotional reads. A MEMORY AWAY...from danger, from passion...from love!

Charlotte Douglas knows about emotion. Her heroes always make us feel loved. But this author of several Harlequin American Romance novels and Harlequin Intrigue books has never forgotten her high school sweetheart—she married him three decades ago!

We hope you enjoy this and all the special amnesia books in the A MEMORY AWAY... program.

Sincerely,

Debra Matteucci

Senior Editor & Editorial Coordinator
Harlequin Books
300 East 42nd Street
New York, NY 10017

A Woman
of Mystery
Charlotte Douglas

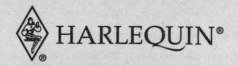

HARLEQUIN®

TORONTO • NEW YORK • LONDON
AMSTERDAM • PARIS • SYDNEY • HAMBURG
STOCKHOLM • ATHENS • TOKYO • MILAN • MADRID
PRAGUE • WARSAW • BUDAPEST • AUCKLAND

ISBN 0-373-22515-6

A WOMAN OF MYSTERY

This edition published by arrangement with Harlequin Books S.A.

® and TM are trademarks of the publisher. Trademarks indicated with ® are registered in the United States Patent and Trademark Office, the Canadian Trade Marks Office and in other countries.

Look us up on-line at: http://www.romance.net

Printed in U.S.A.

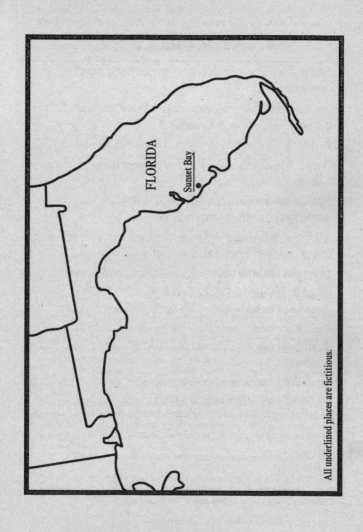

FLORIDA

Sunset Bay

All underlined places are fictitious.

CAST OF CHARACTERS

"Angel"—She's stalked by a past she can't remember.

Jordan Trouble—An ex-cop whose past and present live up to his name.

David Swinburn—A man without a future.

Frank Maricosso and Sidney Stepman—Hired killers.

Henry and Fiona Erskine—Employees at Swinburn's waterfront mansion.

Michael Winslow—An attorney who tries to keep a woman with amnesia out of jail.

Maggie Henderson—A detective, nicknamed Mighty Mouse, who's on the trail of a killer.

James Lassiter—David Swinburn's real estate partner.

Bunny Shelton—David Swinburn's accommodating secretary.

Carleton James—A millionaire whose money comes from unknown sources.

Chapter One

Jordan Trouble spotted her the instant she walked into the tiki bar. It wasn't every night a class act in a white linen suit rubbed elbows with the tourists at Mary Tiger's bar on Sunset Bay Beach.

Vacationing college girls in wispy bikinis and clinging wet T-shirts, middle-aged grandmothers stuffed in too-tight Bermuda shorts and blue-haired, sun-dried retirees sporting floral shifts and flip-flops often drifted through, but this stunning blonde stood out from the typical midnight crowd like a flower in a sandspur patch.

Jordan leaned back on a rattan stool at the far corner of the bar to enjoy the view—until his police training kicked in and made him notice details.

The classy blonde moved with easy grace, but she cast anxious glances over her shoulder and tugged nervously at a gold hoop earring, marring her poise, which at first glance had seemed flawless. Where thick lashes swept her pale cheeks, violet shadows suggested exhaustion or illness, and wrinkles crisscrossed her expensive suit, as if she'd slept in it.

The sudden tightening in his lower body surprised him. He had believed those responses dead.

Like the rest of him.

That his unexpected reaction included more than simple lust startled him most of all. The woman's vulnerability had awakened his protective urge and a rampant curiosity. He wanted to buy her a drink and talk to her, then catalog the features of her attractive oval face, follow the graceful movements of her slender hands and absorb the music of her voice as she answered.

The woman *interested* him.

He grinned with satisfaction. Maybe he wasn't dead after all.

Mary Tiger, the plump Seminole bartender in a voluminous muumuu, refilled his club soda and added a wedge of lime. Her obsidian eyes followed his gaze and glistened with humor above nut-brown cheeks and a broad, toothy smile. "She a friend of yours?"

He shook his head at the warmhearted woman who had rescued him from the brink of self-destruction a few months earlier. "She's a knockout, but definitely a high-class knockout. Outta my league."

"Why?" Mary Tiger asked, huffy in his defense. "Ain't nothin' wrong with you—'cept a smart mouth and the occasional blues."

"A woman like that wouldn't look twice at someone like me," he teased, "who earns only the meager pittance you pay for providing security."

"Security?" Mary Tiger's derisive snort wiggled

her double chins, but affection lighted her eyes. "Damn fancy name for a bouncer."

With amazing grace for a woman of her dimensions, Mary Tiger moved to the opposite end of the bar. She plopped a paper cocktail napkin on the teakwood surface in front of the blonde, who was perched on a stool as if ready to take flight. As Jordan watched, the newcomer mouthed a question, and Mary Tiger jerked her thumb backward, toward him.

The blonde's gaze met his for an instant. Fear shone in her luminous eyes, but he read strength in the tilt of her chin and determination in the set of her jaw. The attractive, mysterious woman so captivated him, he didn't notice two new arrivals until they had maneuvered to either side of her. As out of place as the well-dressed blonde, the strangers in dark business suits squeezed her between them.

Without success, she attempted to pull from their grasp, and the sudden terror in her expression transmitted clearly to Jordan's end of the bar.

Menace crackled in the air like an electrical current, and he tensed. At Mary Tiger's, any problem immediately became his problem, and the situation at the far end of the bar had disaster written all over it.

He sighed. Of all the tiki bars in all the world, why did she have to walk into this one?

The taller man had clamped the blonde's right arm in a viselike grip, and the other had seized her left elbow. Between them, they lifted her from the bar stool and half carried her toward the streetside exit.

They approached Jordan's end of the bar, and her frightened gaze caught his. Panic had drained the color from her face.

"Help me." Her lips moved in a silent plea, and her fear-glazed eyes echoed her silent request.

Reacting automatically, he slid from the bar stool, paced three long strides toward the door and turned. When the trio reached him, he greeted the unfamiliar suits in a low, easy voice. "Looks like the lady doesn't want to go with you."

The taller man contorted weasel-like features in a scowl. "What the *lady* wants isn't your business. Get out of our way."

She stepped toward Jordan. "Please—"

The shorter man jerked her back, silencing her low, husky voice.

"Yeah," the short guy said, "the lady says please leave us alone. This ain't got nothing to do with you."

"Maybe you're right." Jordan shrugged and pivoted away.

Using the momentum of his turn, he wheeled back toward the trio and smashed his fist into the tall man's jaw. Releasing the woman, the weasel went down like a building in a demolition blast. When Jordan seized the short man by his cheap tie and lifted him to his toes, he, too, let the blonde go.

"Now—" Jordan unhanded shorty and stepped back "—either you and your pal clear out and leave the lady alone, or I call the cops."

As the short man adjusted his tie, his coat bulged,

revealing an automatic in a shoulder holster. Jordan reached to his own back, but his hand closed over air where his weapon should have been. He hadn't carried a gun in over a year, and the memory lapse cost him.

His opponent, taking advantage of Jordan's hesitation, shoved the woman away and slammed him above the eyebrow with a solid left hook. Jordan reeled from the blow, but quickly regained his balance and blinked a trickle of blood from his eye. His blurred gaze swept the now-quiet room.

The dazed blonde had landed among a tangle of overturned chairs and remained slumped against the leg of a table. Beside her, the weasel had risen as far as his knees before Mary Tiger loomed over him with the Louisville Slugger she kept behind the bar.

"Go ahead." She choked the bat like a pro stepping up to the plate. "Make my day."

Aware of the weapon in the short man's coat, Jordan said calmly, "Take your friend and get out, and we'll forget this ever happened."

The short guy, suddenly alert to the attentive crowd, averted his face from the curious group. "Let's go, Frank. Too damn many witnesses."

After a searing glance at the unconscious woman beneath the table, Frank followed his partner out the door, and they disappeared at a trot into the early morning darkness.

Jordan knelt beside the stunned woman and brushed hair like pale gold off her colorless face. "You okay?"

Her eyelids fluttered briefly but didn't open.

Concerned by her unnatural stillness, he lifted her in his arms. In contrast to her cool appearance, a seductive heat radiated from her body.

"Call 911, Mary Tiger. We need police and paramedics."

Mary Tiger set her lips in a stubborn line and shook her head. "Don't want *no* police. And 'less she's hurt bad, no paramedics. They call the cops."

He nodded. After a near riot started by spring-breakers a week ago, Mary Tiger worried about losing her liquor license. After all she'd done for him, he couldn't put her in a jam. As much as he disliked the obligation, the blonde was now his responsibility.

"Call Doc Martin to meet me at my boat. Tell him to bring his bag."

He shifted the woman in his arms, stepped out into the night and checked the deserted street for any sign of the two strangers. The only movement he spotted was a night heron, straggling through the sand-strewn parking lot toward the deserted fishing pier.

The humid air was heavy with salt spray and the fragrance of lemon blossoms and bougainvillea. Beyond the bar's cypress poles and thatched-palm roof, the Gulf of Mexico glittered in the moonlight along a sugar-sand beach.

Regret shuddered down his spine. Last year on a night like this, his life had ended. Sure, he still walked and breathed, but his soul had died that April night beneath a waning moon and an onshore breeze.

Memories prompted a craving that twisted viciously in his gut. He thought longingly of the bottle of Absolut vodka, its unbroken seal a symbol of his victory, that sat in a galley cabinet of his boat. After finally accepting that drinking only weakened his defenses against unbearable memories, with Mary Tiger's support, he had conquered that devil six months ago. He couldn't fall off the wagon now if he intended to aid the woman in his arms.

And he couldn't let her down. His nightmare had begun when he failed another woman a year ago. Helping the blonde might begin to atone for his fatal mistake.

Cradling her against his chest, he set off across the boulevard toward the marina.

HER HEAD HURT.

And she was floating, wrapped in a firm, warm cloud that pulsated beneath her cheek. Cool air, laden with the sharp bite of salt spray, caressed her skin and the rhythmic crash of distant surf soothed her.

She was safe.

She relaxed and surrendered again to the blackness.

Later—she'd lost all track of time—a blinding light intruded on her darkness. She squeezed her eyelids against it, but steady fingers pried them open.

The light flicked off, the hands released her and she closed her eyes again.

Gentle fingers traced her scalp, and she flinched when they touched the spot where her head ached.

''Nothing's broken,'' a voice like snow tires on a

smooth road announced. "Just a bad bump on the noggin. Could be a slight concussion, so keep a close eye on her."

"That will be a pleasure." Unlike the roughness of the first, this voice resonated like hot-buttered rum. Smooth and rich with a hint of laughter. Reassuring.

She drifted back into nothingness, vaguely conscious of rocking like a baby to the lullaby of water lapping against a wall.

Sometime later, she stretched in the narrow confines of an unfamiliar bed and opened her eyes. Through the window beside her, streaks of pink and gold stained a forest of defoliated trees.

Sunrise or sunset?

And where was she?

She bolted upright in a rapid movement that blurred her vision and shot slivers of pain through her head.

"Whoa, take it easy." Someone eased her backward against a nest of soft pillows on a sofa.

She gazed up at the owner of the buttered-rum voice. Her eyes focused on his familiar face, and she wondered how she could have forgotten the name of the man with midnight-blue eyes that seemed to bore straight through her. A faint stubble of beard shadowed the craggy lines of his square jaw, and thick brown hair, burnished gold with sun streaks, spilled across his brow as he leaned above her, his appealing mouth fixed in a concerned frown.

She tore her gaze from the mesmerizing blue eyes

and nodded toward the trees outside the window. "Where am I?"

"Sunset Bay Marina."

She blinked, and the defoliated trees transformed into sailboat masts.

"I'm on a *boat?* How did I get here?"

"I carried you from Mary Tiger's bar." He nodded toward the west. "Across the boulevard on the beach."

She didn't remember. Lifting her hand, she examined her throbbing scalp. As she probed her aching head with cautious fingers, her sense of safety evaporated, and her heart thudded with alarm.

"Was I hurt *before* or *after* you brought me here?"

He stepped away, but not before a look of disappointment flitted across his attractive face. "I saved you from a couple of kidnappers. Don't you remember?"

Standing on the threshold of sliding doors that opened to a deck at the cabin cruiser's stern, he almost filled the frame with his broad, tanned shoulders. He wore nothing but white denim shorts slung low on narrow hips, canvas deck shoes and a devil-may-care smile.

Maybe the bump on her head had skewed her reasoning, but she figured he wasn't the one who had harmed her.

Until she spotted the blood on her jacket.

She scrambled to a sitting position, prepared to flee. "What—"

"Don't panic." He returned inside, pulled a folding director's chair next to the sofa and sat beside her. "That's my blood, not yours."

"*Your* blood?" Her fear escalated. He had to be lying. His bare muscular torso and long, sturdy legs displayed no wound, although a small pink scar, long healed, blossomed like a rosette in the sun-bronzed skin above his left collarbone. "You don't look hurt."

He shoved the hair off his forehead to reveal several fresh stitches in the brow above his left eye. "Doc Martin sewed me up after he checked you over."

His sympathetic manner warmed her and eased her fear. He had come to her aid and been wounded in the process. She traced his injured brow lightly with her fingertip. "You were hurt on my account, and I don't even know your name."

He jerked as if her touch had burned him, then stood and crossed into the galley, where he filled a coffeemaker reservoir with water and scooped grounds into the filter-lined basket. "My name's Jordan."

"I'm indebted to you, Mr. Jordan—"

"Jordan's my first name." He flashed a self-deprecating grin. "My last name's Trouble."

Her mind fogged, as if she were dreaming and unable to force herself awake. Nothing about the morning seemed real, including the name of her rescuer. "Trouble? You're kidding."

"Nope." His grin remained, but pain and an unbearable sadness seemed to flicker behind the dark blue eyes. "People who know me say it's a fitting description."

He plunged his head into a counter-high refrigerator and removed bacon, eggs and a carton of orange juice. When he confronted her again, the misery in his eyes had disappeared. She guessed the look of elusive suffering had been a trick of light and not pain after all.

"What's your name?"

My name?

The hovering blackness, the yawning emptiness she'd struggled to ignore swept over her, swallowing her in its terrifying void.

"Hey!" He rushed to her side. "You've gone as pale as that sheet. I'd better call Doc Martin."

She grasped his hands and clung to him. "No, I'll be okay—"

The woman's voice cracked, and she stifled a sob. *Aw, damn.*

At her tears, Jordan felt the noose of responsibility tighten around his neck. He was beginning to care what happened to her. A very bad sign.

With reluctance counterbalancing pleasure, he drew her against his chest and smoothed her silky hair. "Go ahead and cry if it makes you feel better. Last night must have been a nightmare."

She wept quietly, and her soft cheek and the track of her tears warmed the bare skin of his chest. He fought against the desire to shield her from unpleasantness. He'd had that protective feeling before, and it had led to a disaster he'd been helpless to pre-vent—a violent death.

The greatest kindness he could show this woman was to send her away, back to loved ones who could protect her as he couldn't. He pulled away from her and yanked a handful of tissues from a box on the end table.

"Wipe your eyes." The sharp sting of memories laced his voice with unintended harshness. "Then give me a phone number, and I'll call someone to come for you."

Her lips trembled at his suggestion, and her fore-head wrinkled.

Sorry for the roughness of his command, he gripped her chin gently between thumb and forefin-ger, tilted her face upward and dabbed at her tears. Her skin had retained its smooth perfection, even when she cried, and he regretted not meeting her at another time and place, before his world had cracked apart.

She offered him a wavering smile and took the tissues. Gradually her trembling ceased, and she blew her nose with a daintiness that made him smile.

"I'm sorry," she said. "I didn't mean to weep buckets all over you."

"The important thing is to get you home."

Her eyes brimmed with fresh tears. "You don't understand."

Aw, hell, here it comes.

He was being sucked into a situation he should avoid like fifty miles of bad road, but he'd have to be a corpse not to feel sympathy for her. "Maybe if you explain—"

"I can't remember." Horror edged her voice.

He draped his arm around her and gave her quivering shoulder a consoling pat. "Last night was a bad experience. It's best you *don't* remember."

Her gold-flecked brown eyes filled with panic, and she wriggled from his grip. "But I don't remember *anything.*"

Jordan blinked. "Nothing?"

"Not even my own name."

Biting back a curse, he shoved his fingers through his hair. Attractive and vulnerable as she was, his intention had been to unload this beautiful dilemma as soon as possible. Amnesia threw an unexpected kink into his plan.

She surveyed the lounge of his cabin cruiser in a desperate search. "Didn't I have a purse, a wallet, *something* with identification?"

He recalled her graceful stride as she'd entered the bar, one hand at her side, the other tugging at her earring. "You weren't carrying anything last night, unless you have something in your pockets."

She patted the breast and side pockets of her suit jacket. Her eyes relayed her disappointment, but her chin jutted defiantly. "Nothing."

He silently applauded her courage. He doubted most people would hold together as well if their memories had been obliterated. "Doc Martin said to call if there was any change. I'd say loss of memory is enough for him to want another look at you."

She glanced at the clock above his television. "His office won't open for hours."

"He's just a few minutes away."

"A doctor who makes house calls?" She stared in disbelief.

"He's retired. Lives on his yacht across the harbor."

She struggled to her feet and balanced on wobbly legs. "I must have had a car. Or if I came in a taxi, maybe the driver will remember me. I can't wait for the doctor."

Common sense screamed to let her go, but his conscience wasn't listening. He sat and tugged her onto the sofa beside him. Obviously still suffering from the blow to her head, she didn't protest.

"You can't go wandering into the street without ID and your clothes covered in blood. There's no telling where you'd end up."

She exhaled a sigh of defeat and leaned against the back of the sofa. Her hair cascaded over the twill fabric like a waterfall of sunshine.

"Okay," she relented. "Call the doctor."

He reached for his cell phone. "You can shower while I fix breakfast. I'll lend you some clothes."

HOT WATER STUNG her bruised scalp, but the pulsing stream rejuvenated her, and as she dried herself with the oversize, fluffy towel in the boat's tiny head, she felt almost normal.

Except she hadn't a clue who she was.

At first, the not knowing had petrified her, but now

the terror had receded, and she floated in a peaceful limbo free of stress, fears and obligations, her mind a clean slate.

Avoiding the tender spot on her head, she toweled her hair, then wiped steam from the mirror. The face that stared back seemed familiar, but she couldn't put a name to it.

Hoping the doctor could provide a speedy remedy, she stepped into stonewashed denim shorts borrowed from Jordan and cinched the leather belt to secure the too-big waist. She unfolded the soft and faded navy T-shirt, and Sunset Bay Police Department jumped out at her in three-inch, Day-Glo yellow letters.

Apprehension, activated by the word *police,* paralyzed her. Her chest tightened, her breath labored, and her palms turned wet. An illogical urge to bolt overcame her, and she would have fled—but she couldn't move.

Without recollections, she had no explanation for her anxiety. She tried to convince herself she was lucky she'd wound up with a police officer instead of a serial killer, but some latent instinct, not scoured blank like her memories, sent her heart thumping with fear and shattered her earlier composure to smithereens.

Why was she afraid of the police?

Only criminals feared the police.

But she wasn't a criminal.

Was she?

The nameless face in the mirror provided no answer. Shaking off her paralysis, she tugged on the shirt and stepped into the galley. The aroma of fresh coffee and sizzling bacon greeted her.

Jordan placed a heaped plate on the table across from the minuscule galley. "If you feel like eating, Doc said breakfast would be the best thing for you. He'll be here within the hour."

She scooted onto the vinyl-covered bench. Through the wide window that contoured the cabin, she gazed past boats moored alongside and studied the unfamiliar bar across the street, built like a Seminole *chickee* with cypress poles and a roof of dried palm fronds. Her frustration swelled at recognizing a *chickee* but not knowing her own name.

To hide her tension, she sipped orange juice while Jordan filled his plate at the stove. "Why did you bring me here last night?"

"For Doc to take a look at you."

"Why not take me to a hospital? Since when does a police officer take his work home?"

With his back to her, he ceased all movement. "I'm not a police officer."

His sudden quietness and colorless tone disturbed her as much as her irrational surge of relief. "You just collect T-shirts?"

He crossed the galley and slid onto the bench across from her. The muscles of his face were impassive, but a turmoil of emotion filled eyes as dark as a moonless sky.

"I used to be a cop. Until I almost bought the farm," he said in a voice as distant as his expression.

Her gaze flew to the puckered scar below his shoulder. A bullet wound. "Why didn't you call the police last night?"

Sipping his coffee, he eyed her over the rim of his cup. "I work as a bouncer for Mary Tiger. When you came in last night, two thugs tried to haul you out against your will."

"And you intervened?"

"That's my job."

"And these two…thugs?"

"They left."

"Does your job description include bringing home strays?"

"Not exactly."

Her anxiety resurfaced. Did he somehow *know* she was frightened of the police? "Why didn't you call the cops?"

"Look, lady—"

"My name's not *lady*."

"Then what is it?" He arched an eyebrow.

She clenched her hands on the table. "I don't know."

He reached across and smoothed a callused palm over her fist. "I have to call you something."

His touch was oddly reassuring, and at the compassion in his voice, tears prickled her eyes. "I've always detested Jane Doe, but how I can remember *that* and not my own name beats me."

Rubbing the stubble on his chin, he leaned back and contemplated her with a twinkle in his eyes. "You're definitely not a Jane. When I saw you enter the bar last night, dressed in white, long golden hair…'' He grinned as an idea hit him. ''I'll call you Angel.''

She fidgeted and flushed under his scrutiny. ''Doesn't Angel sound a bit…poetic?''

''It fits.'' He squeezed her hand and released it. ''And it's only temporary. Doc will have you fixed up in no time, and you'll have your real name back.''

JORDAN HAD BEEN overly optimistic about Doc Martin's abilities.

The old man had proclaimed Angel apparently physically fit, but suffering from amnesia induced by either the blow to her head or psychological trauma. He prescribed a visit to the emergency room for tests and a second opinion.

Angel refused.

''You should do what he says,'' Jordan insisted after the doctor had left. ''You could have a concussion.''

She shook her head, and fear flashed in her eyes. ''Almost being kidnapped by the characters you described is enough to make anyone want to forget.''

He considered the possibility she was faking amnesia to gain his help and a hideout from the men who were after her. But remembering the depth of her terror when she'd tried to recall her name, he discarded the idea. Unless she was an incredible actress, she couldn't have bluffed that well.

''Let me take you to the station for fingerprinting.

With their new computers, the police can identify you in a matter of minutes.''

"No." Her flat refusal reverberated loudly in the closed confines of the cabin. "No police."

His suspicions sprang back to life. "Why not?"

Anguish and indecision marked her lovely face. "I don't know. Instinct warns me to avoid them."

Her expression, both puzzled and frightened, evoked a tenderness that was sure to steer him smack into disaster. He reined in his galloping emotions. The sooner he found out who she was, the sooner he could pass responsibility for her to someone else.

"Let me earn my keep." She began to clear the breakfast table. "I'll do dishes."

While Angel ran water in the galley sink, he grabbed his napkin from the table, wrapped her empty juice glass in it and slipped the bundle into the pocket of his windbreaker on the bench beside him. Anticipating this move, he had wiped away his own prints before filling her glass.

"I'll check the parking lot at Mary Tiger's and the surrounding streets for a car ticketed from last night."

She turned from the sink and pushed back her hair, leaving a puff of soapsuds across one cheek. "I hadn't thought of that."

"You're not a cop."

Her eyes widened with alarm. "Ex-cop."

"Right."

"And if you don't find a ticketed car?"

"I'll contact the cab and rental car companies—

after I've taken a Polaroid shot of you for identification purposes." He shrugged into his jacket.

Her smile was tentative. "If I had to lose my memory, it looks like I came to the right place."

CONFLICTING EMOTIONS battled inside Jordan as he climbed into his ten-year-old Volvo and drove four short blocks to the Sunset Bay Police Department's beach substation. Mingling with his urge to protect her came his reluctance to get involved for fear of screwing up.

Again.

Not to mention that he was doing exactly what she'd begged him not to.

When he reached the station, he discovered Hal Walden on desk duty. His old buddy greeted him with the same tired joke. "What a way to start the morning. First thing to walk in the door is Trouble."

Jordan tugged the wrapped glass from his pocket. "Remember the time I saved your life and you claimed you'd always owe me?"

Hal folded long arms on the desk and bent his tall, lanky frame to meet him eye to eye. "And I meant it. What do you need?"

Jordan unwrapped the glass. "You'll find a set of prints on this. I need to know the name of the woman who belongs to them."

"Woman?" Hal sniffed the contents of the glass, and the contours of his narrow face lifted in a leering grin. "You had breakfast with a chick you don't even know?"

"It's a long story and not even close to what you're thinking."

"How do you know what I'm thinking?"

"I know *you*, Hal, and you've been a dirty old man since you were three."

Hal grinned without denial. Then his expression sobered. "I have to log on to the computer to check these. What if I come up with a hit?"

"I doubt you'll find she's wanted for anything. All I need is her name."

Hal wiggled bushy eyebrows and grinned wider. "And address?"

Jordan sighed and struggled for patience with the pal who was doing him a favor. "Yeah, and address."

"I'll call you when I have something."

On his way back to the marina, Jordan toured the municipal parking lots and streets near the bar but spotted no parking tickets to indicate a vehicle had been left overnight. Except for Mary Tiger's pickup in her reserved spot, the bar's private lot was empty. He wanted to question the bar owner but decided to call her after checking on Angel.

An unaccustomed flutter of anticipation rippled through his gut as he strode down the weathered planks of the dock toward his boat. Lack of detachment was not a good sign. He needed to work fast to get the beguiling Angel out of his life.

When he vaulted onto the deck, she met him at the sliding glass door, looking even prettier than he remembered.

"Any luck?" she asked.

He shook his head, and the disappointment on her face hit him like a blow. She followed him inside, curled long, shapely legs beneath her and settled in the corner of the sofa.

Lust, hot and powerful, walloped him at the sight, and he toyed fleetingly with the idea of taking her to bed in his cabin. Hell, he was beginning to think like Hal. Not that Jordan was averse to one-night stands. He'd avoided any deeper involvement for the past year. But only a first-class jerk would take advantage of a woman with no memories, no matter how much of a knockout she was.

He cooled his jets and concentrated on business. "My inquiry hasn't scratched the surface yet. Besides, according to Doc, your memory could return any minute, long before we've exhausted our search."

"Or it could return in bits and pieces—" she drew in a sharp breath "—or not at all. Isn't that what he said?"

He ignored a yearning to draw her into his arms. "The worst-case scenario seldom happens. I have something else to try before we tackle the cab and rental car companies."

He opened a cabinet built into the bulkhead and retrieved his cell phone from its charger.

Angel jumped to her feet and grabbed his arm. "You're not calling the police?"

His previous errand stung his conscience. "I'm calling Mary Tiger."

"Why?" She released him, and his skin glowed warm where her hand had been.

"You spoke to her right before your 'friends' arrived. Maybe you told her your name."

He punched in the number of the bar.

Mary Tiger picked up on the first ring. "How's the girl?"

"Okay, except for a slight problem."

"Don't tell me she's going to sue."

He quickly put that fear to rest and asked his questions. When he clicked off the phone, Angel confronted him, eagerness shining in her honey-brown eyes. "Well?"

"You didn't tell her your name."

"But I spoke to her?"

"You asked a question."

He marched to the galley cabinet, withdrew the unopened bottle of Absolut and removed a clean glass from the dish drainer. With a shudder of self-control, he placed bottle and glass on the counter and turned his back on them.

"Don't make me drag it out of you." Her throaty voice rose an octave. "What did I say to the woman?"

Abandoning the galley and the vodka, he sank into a chair and stared at Angel with a gut-wrenching sensation of inevitability.

"You asked her where to find *me*."

Chapter Two

"I was looking for *you?*" Angel's eyes grew round with surprise.

"That's what Mary Tiger said."

"That's rich," she said with an ironic laugh. "I was looking for Trouble. Well, I certainly found it."

"The question is why, why me?"

She squinted suspiciously. "Are you sure you don't know who I am?"

"I never laid eyes on you before last night."

And believe me, a woman as gorgeous as you, I would have remembered.

She leaned back on the sofa and stretched out her legs. "If we can figure out why I was looking for you, maybe we can work backward and figure out who I am."

Jordan pulled his gaze from her long, tanned legs, the perfection of her bare feet and the delicate shell-pink of her toenails. The sight had him struggling to remember his own name. "There're only so many reasons a person goes looking for someone."

"Maybe you owe me money?" she suggested.

He shook his head. "I know the people I owe. You're not one of them."

"I wanted to borrow money?"

"Wrong again. Anyone who knows me also knows I'm broke. And from the cut of the clothes you're wearing, I'd say lack of money isn't your problem."

She frowned. "It is now. I don't have a cent to my unknown name."

He flashed a reassuring smile. "I'm not so broke I can't afford a guest—for a while. We'll worry about your finances later."

"Maybe I'm a long-lost relative."

"I hope not." Not with the thoughts running through his head.

"You could do worse for relatives," she said testily.

"But you couldn't. I'm Trouble, remember?"

Her defensiveness vanished. "Maybe I wanted you to work for me."

"As a bouncer? Sorry, but you don't strike me as the type who owns a bar."

She tunneled her fingers through her long blond hair and lifted it off her neck. "None of this makes sense. I'm scared of the police, but I walk into a strange—at least, I assume it's strange—bar and ask for an ex-cop. Why?"

He shrugged. "If you knew those two goons were on your trail, you could have been looking for help."

"What kind of help?"

"Protection."

Alarm glimmered in her eyes. "Oh."

"You could know somebody who knows me, who figured I'd be happy to earn a few bucks—"

"Doing what?" She eyed him suspiciously.

"Security work, a bodyguard. You didn't think I'd hire out as a hit man?"

She squirmed as if he'd read her thoughts. "I don't remember much, but I know violence is against my nature. I would never hire a hit man."

"This discussion is leading us nowhere. It's time to check the taxi and rental car—"

The cell phone buzzed in his hand. When he answered, he could barely make out Hal Walden's voice. "I can't hear you. Speak up."

"I can't," Hal said. "I'm taking a chance calling you from the station as it is."

"What's up?"

"Jeez, man, thanks to you and your favors, I'm neck-deep in manure."

"Just for logging on the computer? Don't give me that."

"Will you listen!" Hal shouted. "I need some help here." He dropped his voice and Jordan strained to hear. "I ran those prints through the Automated Fingerprint Identification System."

"That's good." Jordan waved Angel a thumbs-up. "What's her name?"

"It's *not* good," Hal said with a groan. "She wasn't in AFIS, but when they find out who she is, there'll be a warrant out for her arrest."

Jordan bolted upright in his chair. "What?"

"For breaking and entering on Turtle Key before midnight last night."

Angel, a cat burglar?

"Her prints," Hal said, "match those the crime scene unit lifted from a jimmied front door and inside the house."

Avoiding Angel's puzzled look, Jordan stepped onto the deck at the stern of the boat and closed the sliding glass door behind him. "Anything stolen?"

"No." Hal's breath whistled through his teeth. "Man, my neck is on the block. The detectives will want to know where I got that print. How am I going to explain?"

"Let me think."

Jordan paced for several long minutes while seagulls wheeled and screeched overhead.

"Okay, here's what you do. Take the juice glass to the property room, tell them you found it and a copy of the prints beside the computer."

"But what about my log-on code?"

"If anybody asks, say you assumed the detectives wanted an AFIS report. Otherwise, don't mention it."

"That might get me off the hook," he said grudgingly, "but what are you going to do about the woman?"

Jordan's thoughts raced. Turning Angel over to the cops would take her off his hands. He glanced into the cabin, where she watched him through the glass door with curiosity etched all over her unforgettable face. Not the face of a criminal. He'd bet his boat on that.

If he handed her over to the law, without her memories, she'd have no way to defend herself against any charges. The prospect of Angel behind bars prodded his conscience. He'd be a first-class jerk to desert her now.

"Trouble? You still there?"

"Yeah, and I'm not going to turn her in."

"Man, are you crazy?" Hal breathed heavily into the phone, as if he'd run a foot race.

"Probably. So you don't know her name?"

"No clue. And if you don't bring her in, you could be charged with obstruction. Hell, *I* could be charged."

"I know what I'm doing, Hal. She's not a criminal, and like you said, nothing was stolen. I want to get to the bottom of this before I tell the police about her. Give me the name and address of the folks who had the break-in."

"I'm already in enough hot water—"

"Give, or should I tell the chief it was you last year who accidentally blasted that hole in the new cruiser roof with the riot gun?"

"But I didn't—"

"I can be very convincing."

Hal hesitated, then mumbled the information. "But you didn't hear it from me."

"Thanks, buddy. I owe you." Jordan pocketed the phone and went back into the cabin.

"Was that call about me?" Angel asked.

"I have a lead on your identity, but to follow up, I'll need you to trust me."

Her expression turned wary. "Trust you how?"

"I'm going out for a while, and I want you to stay inside, out of sight, until I return."

Fear replaced her guarded look. "That phone call—those men are back, aren't they?"

"Yes," he lied. She'd be more likely to consent to his plan if she believed her almost abductors had returned.

"Okay," she agreed, white-faced.

What kind of a jerk are you? First you ask her to trust you, then you lie to her, right off the bat. If the woman had any sense, she'd start running and not stop until she reached the next state.

And if you had any sense, you'd let her.

He crossed the lounge, seized the vodka bottle and with superhuman effort stashed it out of sight again in the galley cabinet.

Unable to shake the cloud of predestined calamity that hovered over him, he brushed past her, leapt from the boat and sprinted down the dock toward his car.

FOR TWO HOURS, Angel paced the lounge, waiting for Jordan's return. Fear of encountering the men he claimed had tried to kidnap her kept her inside, even when the confines of the forty-foot boat made her claustrophobic.

But more than fear held her there.

After piecing together the fragments Jordan had

told her, she realized she was in some kind of danger, and she suspected she had sought out Jordan Trouble to protect her. Somehow, irrationally perhaps, she believed staying with him kept her safe.

To be honest, she had to admit she remained in Jordan's company for more than safety. Right now, he was the only friend she had.

What she had first mistaken for attraction sizzling between them *had* to be gratitude for his rescue, even though Jordan's rugged good looks and heart-melting smile would turn the head of any woman.

But a man was more than muscles and a handsome face. She had witnessed his contest with the vodka bottle, a battle he had won—this time. She wondered whether being wounded in the line of duty had launched his struggle with alcohol or if the stresses of police work had driven him to drink long before he'd been shot.

Examining her surroundings, she searched for clues to unlock the secrets of Jordan Trouble's personality. Low shelves, crammed to overflowing with well-worn books, lined the lounge and formed a half wall between the living area and the galley. A scan of the titles revealed Jordan's eclectic taste, from oceanography and history to Tom Clancy's novels and several bestselling mysteries.

She pulled out a narrow, unidentifiable volume to check its title and discovered an official rule book for soccer. A color photograph and a greeting card slipped from its pages to the floor. She retrieved the items and examined the picture in which a group of happy-faced young boys in purple-and-black soccer uniforms gathered around a sign that read Sunset Bay Sizzlers, Police Athletic League. Coach Jordan Trouble.

Flashing his carefree smile, Jordan stood at the far left of the back row, a soccer ball tucked on his cocked right hip, his left hand resting on the shoulder of the boy beside him. He looked cheerful, without his present shadow of despair.

She tucked the photograph back inside the rule book and glanced at the greeting card. More than a dozen children's signatures with special notes to their wounded coach filled the inside. She recalled the saying, *If kids and animals like you, you can't be all bad.* Judging from their messages, the kids had obviously loved Coach Trouble. She smiled and wondered if he'd ever owned a dog.

She continued her search but spotted no other photographs, none of Jordan's family or his former police colleagues, no indication of how he spent his time when he wasn't working in the bar across the street.

Besides his books, the only other clue to his interests was a harmonica, stashed in a handy cubbyhole beside the television. The instrument conjured up images of Jordan, a solitary figure, adrift on his boat in the endless gulf, his haunting melodies carried on the sea breeze. Unlike her, he had his memories, but he seemed more alone than she was.

A desire to ease his isolation gripped her, and she slumped onto the sofa and cradled her still-throbbing head in her hands. Her response to Jordan was irrelevant. For all she knew, even though she wore no rings, she could be married or engaged. A husband or lover could be searching frantically for her at this very minute.

A yawning emptiness, a yearning for *someone* gnawed inside her like an unhealed wound. Her arms ached to hold someone. But for whom was she longing?

Her gaze fell on the day's edition of the *Tribune* lying on the coffee table. She could contact the newspapers and the television stations, explain her situation and ask them to run her picture. Surely somebody out there would recognize her and tell her who she was.

The two who tried to kidnap me know who I am.

But she couldn't alert the police.

Why not?

In frustration, she pounded her fists against her thighs. If Jordan didn't return soon, she would lose what little of her mind she had left.

She shoved to her feet, stomped to the sliding door and gazed toward the parking lot. At the sight of Jordan, sauntering down the dock with two large shopping bags in hand, she had to restrain herself from racing to meet him.

By the time he entered the cabin, she was seated on the sofa, outwardly calm, flipping idly through a magazine, while her pulse galloped at a hundred miles per hour.

Jordan dropped the bags on the floor. "I think I have everything you need."

"Clothes?"

She eyed the packages with annoyance and aversion, but she couldn't explain why Jordan's buying her clothes affected her so negatively. After all, she had nothing to wear but a bloodstained suit, and she didn't dare shop while kidnappers were after her.

"More than clothes," Jordan said with a satisfied smile, evidently unaware of her irritation. "A disguise, so you can leave the boat without being recognized."

Curiosity nudged aside her annoyance. She laid down the magazine to watch him drag out his purchases and arrange them on the coffee table.

When he'd emptied both bags, he selected several items and handed them to her. "Try these on. You can use my cabin. It has a full-length mirror."

Minutes later, she stepped back into the lounge. The white jeans fit her like paint on wood. She'd had to lie flat on the double bed to pull them up and zip them. By contrast, the baggy navy-blue sweatshirt hung low on her thighs, and she shoved the sleeves off her hands. The only things that fit were the socks and running shoes.

Jordan's face lighted with approval. "Perfect."

"That's easy for you to say. These jeans are so tight I can't breathe."

She yelped in surprise when he yanked up the sweatshirt, grabbed her hips and turned her full circle.

"They'll be fine." His strong, capable hands spanned her hips, and his face was too close to hers. "They're denim. They'll stretch."

"Before or after I suffocate?" she demanded, unsure whether to blame her lack of air on the fit of her jeans or the warmth of his hands and the proximity of his lips.

His gaze locked with hers, and heat arced like lightning in the midnight-blue of his eyes before he freed her and turned his attention to the other purchases he'd piled on the table.

She experienced a curious sensation of abandonment and regret when he released her. That knock on the head had damaged more than her memory. It must have short-circuited her brain or she wouldn't have reacted so intensely to a stranger's casual touch.

"Now for the rest." He lifted a straw hat with a four-inch brim and a blue band around the crown. A fall of straight black hair dangled from the inside band. "Try this."

She bundled her hair atop her head, took the hat and eased it over her topknot.

He stepped closer, grasped her chin and turned her head from side to side. The warmth of his breath brushed her cheek, and the pleasing citrus scent of soap filled her nostrils. Again, she struggled to breathe.

"Is it on straight?" she asked, trying to appear unaffected.

With deft fingers, he tucked errant strands of blonde beneath the hat. His face hovered inches from hers, and she closed her eyes against the compelling sight.

"You okay?" He clasped her by the shoulders, and she could feel him staring at her.

Her eyes flew open, and she pulled away and sank onto the sofa. "Just a little dizzy."

Worry wrinkled his brow and darkened his eyes, accentuating his attractiveness. "You had a nasty bump last night—and a bad scare. Maybe you should rest."

"No!"

Her refusal exploded with more force than she'd intended. The best cure for her dizziness was escape from the intimate confines of the boat before she did something stupid, like showing gratitude for Jordan's rescue by throwing herself into his strong, tanned arms.

His concerned expression turned puzzled.

"What I really need is fresh air and a chance to stretch my legs."

"Are you sure?"

She bit back a curt response, blew a strand of nylon hair out of her eyes and nodded.

After another moment of intense scrutiny that made her face flush, he picked up the remaining items and handed them to her. "You'll need the rest of your disguise."

She removed a tube of lipstick from its packaging and frowned. "Reckless Red?"

"The color I thought least likely to suit the real you."

The real me. Whoever that is.

She carried the lipstick to the tiny mirror in the bathroom and smoothed the fiery shade on her lips. Then she slipped on the large-framed dark glasses he'd purchased. A stranger with straight black hair that fell over her shoulders and a slash of brazen color on her mouth stared back at her.

A stranger named Angel.

After a futile attempt to slide the lipstick into the pocket of her too-tight jeans, she set the tube on the shelf above the miniature lavatory, squared her shoulders and returned to the now-empty lounge.

The door to Jordan's cabin was closed, but in a few minutes he emerged, looking more handsome than ever in khaki Dockers, loafers and a dark blue chambray shirt that matched his eyes.

"Ready?" He handed her the clipboard and pen he carried.

"For what?" she asked suspiciously. He had yet to reveal their destination.

His cocky grin made her knees weak as he drew a knuckle gently across her cheek. "To see if we can't jog that stubborn memory of yours."

Torn between her desire to escape the intimacy of the boat and reluctance to expose herself to new dangers, she followed him onto the deck. He bounded to the dock and held out his hand. With his strong grasp steadying her, she leapt the narrow chasm between deck and pier.

As she teetered for balance, her gaze fell on the

name of the boat, painted in flowing black script across the stern, and she laughed aloud at the irony.

Jordan had christened his vessel *Oblivion*.

AFTER A FAST-FOOD LUNCH that Angel only picked at, Jordan turned his Volvo toward the causeway that connected Sunset Bay Beach to the mainland. Halfway across the three-mile span edged with towering palms and beds of tropical flowers, he turned left onto Turtle Key.

Back at the restaurant, Angel had sat huddled in a corner of the booth, obviously fearful of being recognized. Only after fifteen minutes without attracting attention in the crowded room had she relaxed enough for him to coax her to drink her chocolate shake.

Her anxiety had been evident, but it lacked the taint of guilt he had learned to associate with those who disregarded the law. If Angel had broken into that house, he doubted petty thievery had been her goal, not with the air of fresh and open honesty she exuded.

On the other hand, she was undeniably agitated. He suspected something horrible had happened to her—something more than a bump on the head—that had caused her to block her memories. The cop in him wanted to uncover that event.

The *man* in him wanted to understand how this woman had accomplished in a few hours what others had failed to do in months. By reviving his curiosity and his compassion, she'd brought him halfway back to life. He wasn't sure he was grateful.

He'd been alive before, and it had proved too painful.

Driving across the narrow bridge that spanned the canal between Turtle Key and the causeway, he vowed silently to guard against feelings that had caused such agony in the past.

"I want to go back," she announced suddenly.

"Back?"

"To the boat."

Driving slowly and watching street signs for Turtle Way, he cast her a quick glance. She had wrapped her arms around her midriff as if her stomach ached, and her face had paled, a startling contrast to the garish red of her lipstick.

"Do you recognize this area?"

She shook her head. "But it's giving me the willies."

"Good. I—"

"Good! What are you, a sadist?"

He reached over and gently massaged the tensed muscles at the nape of her neck. "If this place disturbs you, it means you've been here before, and we might find clues here to who you are."

She shivered beneath his touch. "What if those men are looking for me here?"

He halted at a four-way stop and studied her to gauge her reaction. "Or the police?"

She closed her eyes. "Please, get me out of here."

"You're in disguise. No one's going to recognize

you. And we may discover your name. Once we do, we'll have a better chance at figuring out why those men are after you. And why you're afraid of the police.''

Guilt at not telling all he knew besieged him, but he needed the element of surprise to jump-start her memory. Doc Martin had mentioned that sometimes a sudden return to familiar surroundings and faces dispelled hysterical amnesia. Jordan figured it was worth a try.

He turned right on Turtle Way and drove slowly down the street, searching for the address.

"I don't think I can do this," she said with a quiver in her voice.

"Sure you can. Just follow the plan we rehearsed. When anyone else is around, keep your head down, your eyes on the clipboard, okay?"

"Okay." But she didn't sound confident.

He eased the car into a circular drive in front of a long, low, contemporary house that hugged the canal behind it, and parked beside a discreet sign by the front door that gave the name of the owners' security service.

He hopped from the car, circled and opened the door for Angel. Cramming her straw hat tightly onto her head, she climbed out. Before she could change her mind and plunge back inside, he quickly shut the door.

"Relax," he said in a low voice, "and leave the talking to me."

With more outward confidence than he felt, he approached the front door. Angel fell in step behind him.

The unpainted new wood of the door frame indicated this was the door that had been jimmied in last night's break-in. He took a deep breath and rang the bell.

A moment later, a lean, sixtyish woman opened the door. With skin leathered by the sun, hair dyed an unnatural red and eyes red-rimmed from crying, she appeared agitated and distraught.

"Mrs. Swinburn?" Jordan asked.

"Yes?" She eyed him with suspicion.

"I'm Joe Cramden from Sovereign Security, and this is Angel, my assistant."

The woman ignored Angel and viewed him with undisguised annoyance. "My husband already spoke with the security service this morning. He's *very* upset that the alarm didn't function last night. We could have been murdered in our beds."

She pressed her hand to her mouth, as if choking back a sob.

"That's why I'm here," Jordan said, improvising. "Your husband spoke with the business office. I'm the technician from the service department. I'll check out the system to determine what went wrong."

"If you'll wait in the living room, I'll get my husband. I can't talk with anyone now. We've had a death in the family."

She opened the door, motioned them inside, then gestured toward the sunken living room on the right. "Wait here. I'll find George."

The woman disappeared down a hall, and Jordan, his hand on Angel's elbow, guided her into an ice-white room filled with furniture in gray leather, chrome and glass. The atmosphere was cold, and not because of the excessive air-conditioning.

The frigid decor's only relief came from a cluster of color photographs on a glass-and-chrome sideboard. Jordan walked closer for a better look at an eight-by-ten wedding portrait in a sterling silver frame. A laughing couple stared back at him. The groom, a stolid man with dark hair, smiled with a warmth that didn't reach his eyes.

Jordan had seen that face before. David Swinburn's photograph had stared up at him from the file of the last investigation he had worked as a cop.

The breathtaking bride that Swinburn clutched in a possessive embrace drew Jordan's thoughts quickly back to the present.

The bride was Angel.

Chapter Three

Hiding his surprise, Jordan glanced at the next picture. It was also of Angel, holding a toddler, a little girl who looked like a miniature copy of herself. Angel had to be the child's mother.

Ignoring the irrational disappointment at learning she had a husband and daughter, he congratulated himself on the prospect of turning her over to the care of her family. After last year's tragedy, he never again wanted responsibility for anyone but himself.

However, he'd have to check out the Swinburns before he revealed Angel's identity. The fact that she'd broken into their house meant her relationship with them had somehow gone awry, and without more information, telling them who she was could prove a nasty mistake.

She tugged at his arm. "We have to go. I can't stay here any longer."

At that moment, George Swinburn, an older version of the groom in the portrait, entered the room. His scowl relayed his displeasure. "I thought I settled everything with Tony this morning. He never mentioned anyone named Cramden. Who *are* you, anyway?''

Before Jordan could answer, Angel raced past him and Swinburn and bolted out the door.

''What the hell is going on?'' Swinburn demanded.

Jordan, itching to make sure Angel didn't disappear, latched onto the first excuse that came to mind. ''My assistant's pregnant. Sometimes her stomach acts up.''

''I don't mean *her*. What's going on with the security system?''

''I'm sorry.'' Jordan thought fast and shifted toward the exit. ''The office didn't tell me about the death in your family. I won't take any more of your time today.''

''Thanks.'' Swinburn accompanied him to the door. ''Just call next time before coming.''

''I'm sorry for your loss.''

Jordan hurried to the car and breathed a sigh of relief at the sight of Angel, scrunched down in the passenger seat, her straw hat askew, covering her profile. At least she hadn't run away.

He climbed inside, started the engine and backed slowly out of the circular drive onto the street. George Swinburn was watching them from his front door, and Jordan didn't want him reading the Volvo's license tag as he drove away.

If he had roused Swinburn's suspicions and the man checked with Sovereign Security, Jordan didn't want to be identified by his car's plates. He might bluff his way out of a jam with his pals in the police department, but he couldn't explain away Angel.

To avoid unwanted attention, he drove at a sedate pace down Swinburn's street and turned onto the causeway. Immediately, he increased speed and headed toward Sunset Bay Beach.

"Feeling better?"

He caught her brief nod from the corner of his eye.

"Did you see the pictures on the sideboard?" he asked casually.

"They—" She drew a deep, shuddering breath. "They looked like me."

"Did they ring any bells?"

"Alarm bells. From the minute we drove onto Turtle Key, I've been shaking like a leaf. The anxiety was worst at that house. That's why I had to get out."

"Did the house or the Swinburns bring back any memories?"

"Nothing—except uneasiness."

Disappointment flooded him. He had hoped she would remember *something*. Enough, at least, that he could hand her over to her relatives with a clear conscience. For all he knew, her kin had set those two thugs on her. "Do you remember your husband? A little girl?"

"I don't want to talk about the pictures or the Swinburns." She angled toward him, and the power of her gaze burned his face. "How did you know to take me there? You *know* who I am, don't you?"

"Not for sure." He purposely ignored her first question. "But I think I've figured it out."

"Who am I?" Her voice vibrated at a sharp, high pitch.

He couldn't just blurt out his suspicions without verifying them first. Besides, her state of mind was already fragile, and he didn't want her going to pieces on him. "We're almost back to the marina—"

"Tell me *now*."

The ring of his phone saved him.

"Be careful," Mary Tiger said in a low voice when he answered. "Those two jerks from last night are here, asking where you live. I told 'em I don't know."

"Thanks—"

"They're asking everybody in the place. Sooner or later someone's gonna tell 'em."

"I should take a little cruise. Can you get someone to cover for me tonight?"

"No problem. But take care of yourself. I didn't sober you up just so you could get yourself killed."

"Mary, love," he said with a smile, "you're getting sentimental in your old age."

"Listen, smart boy," she snapped, but not sharply enough to cover the affection in her voice, "you make sure you *reach* old age, you hear?"

"I'm working on it. And you take care. Those guys are bad news."

He glided the car into its reserved space at the marina, shut off the engine and turned to Angel. "Your would-be kidnappers are back at Mary Tiger's. When you get out of the car, walk straight to the boat and don't look back. I'll be right behind you.''

"But—"

"No time for arguments. Get inside and stay hidden until we've left the marina. Please, just do it.''

Sunglasses didn't hide her apprehension. Her muscles were taut with nervousness as she sprang from the car, slammed the door and hurried down the dock toward the boat. Her long, shapely legs covered the distance quickly, and she disappeared inside.

Jordan reached under the seat for a billed cap, pulled it low over his eyes and removed his dark glasses from the sun visor. With hands in his pockets and shoulders slumped to disguise his height, he slouched across the weathered planks toward the *Oblivion.*

Forcing nonchalance, he disconnected the utility hookups, untied the mooring lines, tossed them on deck and jumped on board. After scampering up the ladder to the flying bridge, he started the engines and backed out of the slip, keeping a sharp eye on Mary Tiger's for any sign of the men who were looking for him. With luck, he'd clear the marina basin and reach the channel before they spotted him and the direction he'd headed.

He jumped at the sudden pressure of a hand on his shoulder.

Angel, still in disguise, stood beside him with the wind blowing fake hair across her cheeks. She removed her dark glasses and, with a lift of her eye-brows, confronted him with unspoken questions.

Fortunately, the roar of the boat's powerful motors prevented conversation and delayed his explanation. As soon as he'd left the no-wake zone, he gunned the engines and headed south into the Intracoastal Waterway.

Traffic in the channel was heavy, and he gave his full attention to piloting his craft. But even as he concentrated on steering the boat, he was aware of Angel beside him.

She had removed the hat and wig, and her long golden hair streamed behind her in the breeze. Her hands gripped the railing lightly for balance. When he glanced at her face, her eyes pierced his soul.

Emotions, long suppressed, stirred and expanded deep inside him, and he fought to bury them again. Over the past year, he had rid his life of sentimental complications, and he worried that the tender and erotic feelings Angel was beginning to arouse in him would undermine his success.

He didn't know the exact nature of her difficulties, but she was in serious trouble, with two apparent kidnappers on her trail and the Sunset Bay police searching for her, as well. He'd be no help to her at all if he let emotion interfere with his instincts and training.

At least he had a fix on her last name now....

Five miles south of Sunset Bay, he shouted to her to resume her disguise, then steered toward the main-land. In a few minutes the boat entered a private marina and dry dock. He pulled alongside a dock by the marina office and killed the engines.

"Why are we stopping?" Angel followed him down the ladder and waited on deck while he secured the lines. "If they find out we're on the water, won't they catch up with us?"

"If we stay on the water, they might." He steadied her as she disembarked. "But I have a few plans to frustrate their efforts."

He headed toward the office, but her hand on his arm stopped him. "You have a lot of explaining to do."

"Let me take care of the boat first." He covered her hand with his. "After that, I'll tell you everything you want to know."

Her sunglasses hid her eyes, but she nodded, and the grim set of her mouth relaxed. She made a point of withdrawing her hand from his grasp. "I really don't have much choice, except to trust you."

Hoping his revelations wouldn't destroy that trust, he hurried into the office.

ANGEL YANKED OFF the itchy hat and wig and tossed them onto the king-size bed of the cramped but clean motel room.

After leaving the office at the private marina, Jordan had hurried her a block down the street to this quaint motel nestled among a stand of Australian pines on the bay. When registering under a false name, he'd requested separate rooms, but with the spring break season still under way, the clerk had only one vacancy.

Once Jordan saw her safely settled, he had gone back to the boat. Darkness had fallen when, carrying not only a flight bag crammed with clothing, but also a cooler filled with food and drinks from the galley, he returned.

"The less we're seen in public—" he set the cooler on a luggage rack "—the better. I also picked up a few items at a Wal-Mart two blocks over."

She had no interest in food or clothes. She wanted facts, and Jordan obviously knew more than he was telling. Jamming her hands on her hips, she confronted him. "What's going on?"

"Nothing."

She refused to allow his electrifying good looks and appealing boyish charm to distract her. "I may have lost my memory, but forgetfulness doesn't make me stupid. I'm tired of being kept in the dark."

His blue eyes clouded with dismay. "If I've held back information, it's only for your protection."

"Protecting me by keeping me ignorant?" she said hotly. "I want facts so I can make my own decisions. Believe me, I *hate* other people deciding for me. David always—"

She stopped cold, puzzled by her own words.

"Who's David?" he asked.

The name had made her dizzy. Weak-kneed, her mind a blank, she sank onto the bed. "I don't know."

"I do."

She jerked her head up in surprise. "Tell me."

He extracted a can of Coke from the cooler, popped the top and offered it to her. When she declined, he settled into an armchair that faced the door and took a drink. "It's a long story, and when you hear it, you're going to be angrier with me than you already are."

"That may not be possible," she said with a wry grimace.

"This morning, I took a glass with your fingerprints to the Sunset Bay police."

"You *what?*" She bounded off the bed, torn between fury and an irrational urge to escape.

"Correct me if I'm wrong," he said with an I-told-you-so grin, "but I think you just got angrier."

"Angry? That doesn't begin to express how I feel." Her emotions emerged white-hot as she stomped the length of the room and back. "How about furious, betrayed and totally ticked off? Those come closer."

He lifted an eyebrow in amusement. "You left out aggravated, annoyed, fuming, irate—"

"I'm just getting warmed up," she snapped.

His infuriating grin didn't waver. "I did it for your own good—"

"How dare you?"

She stopped in front of him, grabbed the arms of his chair and leaned toward him, inches from his face. He didn't retreat. She wanted to shake him and feared she would burst into tears if she didn't cool her anger.

"I *trusted* you." Her voice choked with hurt. "You knew I didn't want the cops involved—I couldn't have made it any clearer—but you ignored my wishes. You're as bad as David—"

The name had caught her once more by surprise. Puzzled by its emergence and her reaction to it, she whirled away from Jordan.

As though a bucket of cold water had been dumped on her, her anger fizzled. Confused, she slumped into the chair opposite him. "What happened at the police station?"

"You don't have anything to worry about. My request was unofficial. A buddy of mine ran your prints through the computer, but the only match that came up was some unidentified prints from a house that was broken into early last night on Turtle Key."

Exhausted, she nodded with comprehension. Their earlier foray finally made sense. "The Swinburns."

"I figure you aren't the cat-burglar type, so you must have broken into their house for another reason. When I took you to Turtle Key this afternoon, I was hoping to jog your memory with familiar faces and surroundings."

She closed her eyes, recalling the anxiety she'd suffered on Turtle Key. And no wonder. She'd returned to the scene of her crime. Her head swam with unanswered questions. "Going there didn't help."

"Not in the way I'd hoped, but the photographs told us something."

"The Swinburns know who I am," she said, stating the obvious.

"And you're related to them in some way. The groom in that wedding portrait looked like a younger version of George Swinburn, maybe a younger brother or a son." His gaze took on laser sharpness. "That makes you either a sister- or daughter-in-law."

"I'm married."

She acknowledged what she'd been trying not to think about since she'd seen the photographs of herself in the Swinburn house. The word *married* sounded alien and made her feel cold and hollow.

"If I can trust the resemblance between you and the child in the photograph," he added gently, "you have a little girl."

Tears filled her eyes and pain flooded her heart. "I have a daughter."

The devastating emptiness that she'd tried to avoid had returned, and she recognized it for what it was— the desire to hold her baby, a little girl she couldn't remember. She didn't know her baby's name and wouldn't know what her child looked like if she hadn't seen the picture.

Yet at the thought of a husband, her emotions had remained unstirred.

"That's all I know," Jordan admitted. "Although I suspect that the David you mentioned is your husband."

No emotion or awareness penetrated her shroud of forgetfulness. "So all I really have is more questions. Why did I break into the Swinburns' house? Where's my daughter? My husband? And why are those men after me?''

Looking guilty, Jordan shifted in his chair.

''You're keeping something back.''

''No.'' His denial came too sharply and quickly.

''Please. Tell me.''

He set down his drink, knelt in front of her and gathered her hands in his with a compassion that brought a lump to her throat. ''All I have are hunches. And hunches aren't always right.''

Insight into his reluctance dawned slowly. ''Mrs. Swinburn said they'd had a death in the family. You think it might have been my husband or—'' Her breath caught and unbearable agony shot through her. ''Or my daughter?''

He pressed her hands, and she returned his strong, warm grip, afraid to let go of the only friend she knew.

''Don't jump to conclusions,'' he said. ''Whoever died could have nothing to do with you. We'll check the obituaries in tomorrow morning's paper.''

Not knowing was torture. ''Sometimes the papers don't report deaths until days later.''

''If it isn't in the paper, I'll call Hal in the morning and ask him to check out who died.''

She nodded. ''We have to deal with what we know—for now.''

His expression of approval chased away some of her chill. ''All we're sure of is that you're connected to the Swinburns and two men are after you. Is it possible they're trying to return you to your family?''

· She shook her head. "Don't ask me how I know, but they're a threat. They don't intend to help me."

He released her hands and returned to his chair. "So, what do you want to do?"

"Do?"

"I can't decide for you, but I'll help if I can. Do you want to keep running? Try to find your husband? Turn yourself in to the cops?"

"No police," she replied abruptly. "I doubt sitting in a cell will help my memory return. But running isn't a solution, either."

Jordan merely nodded.

"If you were me," she said, "what would you do?"

Rubbing his temples, he closed his eyes, apparently lost in thought. Tall and muscular, tanned and self-composed, he appeared indestructible, but she knew better. She'd seen the scar of the bullet wound above his collarbone, less than a hand's width from his heart, and in spite of his veneer of irresistible charm, she had glimpsed the pain in his cobalt-blue eyes.

He had been a gallant rescuer, but also a reluctant one. Why he hadn't turned her in, or at least turned her out, hours ago was a mystery. If the men who pursued her were as dangerous as she suspected, why was Jordan Trouble risking his life for her?

He could have been motivated by his policeman's instincts, but he wasn't a policeman now, and he'd never said why he hadn't returned to the force after his wound healed. He might have taken disability

retirement, but he didn't appear physically incapac-
itated.

She'd heard of cops suffering post-traumatic stress
syndrome from their harrowing experiences on the
street, but the only time Jordan had appeared rattled
was that one brief second when he'd realized she had
lost her memory. Perhaps his brush with death had
turned him into a loner, content with his boat, his
books and his music.

"If I were you," he finally said, "I wouldn't make
any decisions until I had more information."

"Like turning myself in?"

He nodded.

"My husband probably knows all the answers. It
shouldn't be hard to find him."

"We can check the phone book."

Uneasiness clutched her. She couldn't remember
her husband, but she knew she didn't want to see
him.

"The telephone directory will also give us your
address—*if* you still live with him."

"Why wouldn't I?"

"You could be divorced."

"I hadn't thought of that." Divorce might explain
her lack of emotional reaction to her husband and
her reluctance to find him.

"So what will you do now?"

"I want to learn everything I can about myself and
my family. But I can't find out anything if I'm hiding
from the police and those thugs."

''The cops don't know who broke into the Swin-burns' house,'' Jordan reminded her.

''But those two men know *me*.'' She scowled at the wig on the bed with distaste. ''I'll have to stay in disguise.''

He picked up the shopping bag and handed it to her. ''Just a suggestion.''

She opened it and withdrew a pair of scissors, a bottle of dark brown hair dye and a curling iron. Tears tickled the back of her throat. He had recognized how much she had hated that damned wig.

''Drastic times require drastic measures.'' She rose, carried the bag into the bathroom and shut the door.

JORDAN FINISHED HIS soft drink and wrestled with his conscience. The name David Swinburn had opened floodgates to those memories he wanted to forget.

Last year, shortly after adding Swinburn's name to his list of potential suspects, the entire fraud investigation had gone sour, and he'd almost died when his cover was blown. While he recuperated from a bullet in the shoulder, his successors had run into a dead end in their attempts to tie David Swinburn to the statewide real estate scam Jordan had been probing.

Reluctant to add to her worries, he hadn't told Angel about his investigation of her husband. He had no proof against Swinburn, so why prejudice his wife against him?

Jordan was equally hesitant to explain his gut instinct that she was not only in big trouble but major danger. If he attempted to describe the internal radar that had served him well in the past, she'd think he was crazy.

He'd already witnessed too much anxiety in her eyes. Maybe his was a chauvinistic attitude, but he wanted to protect her, not only from danger but from anything that made her unhappy.

Aw, hell. I'm in over my head.

He'd be more useful by remaining neutral, emotionally distant. After less than twenty-four hours with her, he was already beginning to think of her as more than just a luscious body and a gorgeous face.

When Angel stepped out of the bathroom, it was as if he'd been hit by a bolt of lightning. Even in the dim light of the motel room, her extraordinary attractiveness was unmistakable. She hadn't cut or dyed her long blond hair but had twisted it into an elegant French braid. With her hair pulled back from her face, her brown eyes seemed twice as large. And full of apology.

"As much as I hate that wig, I couldn't change my hair. My memories are gone. If I alter my appearance, it's like erasing what little of me is left."

He shrugged in an effort to hide the impact she had on him. "Then you'll have to wear the wig when we leave the room."

"I will, but won't the men who're after us recognize you?"

Before he could answer, his cell phone rang. He grabbed it off the dresser.

"Where are you?" Hal demanded in an angry voice. "I came by the marina and your boat was gone."

"Long story. What's up?"

"All hell broke loose at the station after I talked with you last. Are you near a television?"

Jordan glanced at the ancient' mahogany console in the corner. "In a manner of speaking."

"Turn on Channel 44."

Before Jordan could ask more questions, Hal hung up.

In two strides, Jordan crossed to the set and twisted the dial. The television hummed and took several seconds to warm up before the picture appeared. The anchorwoman was just beginning the ten o'clock news.

He settled into a chair, and Angel, with a puzzled look, perched on the edge of the bed and glued her attention to the set.

"The body of David Swinburn," the anchor announced, "a prominent Sunset Bay real estate agent, was discovered early this morning by his housekeeper in his posh waterfront home."

Film footage of a covered body being wheeled through the wrought-iron gates of a waterfront mansion toward the medical examiner's vehicle scrolled across the screen.

Jordan cast a quick glance at Angel, pale and tight-lipped, then focused on the news.

"Police are releasing no details of the killing but have issued an all points bulletin for the arrest of Sara Swinburn, the deceased's ex-wife."

A color photograph of Angel and the toddler, the same picture he'd seen at the house on Turtle Key, flashed on the screen.

"Sara Swinburn has not been seen since Sunday afternoon," the anchor droned, "and is believed to be traveling with her two-year-old daughter, Brittany, and driving a late-model red Nissan. Anyone with knowledge of Sara Swinburn's whereabouts should call the number on your screen immediately."

Angel turned horror-filled eyes on him. "I'm a murderer."

Chapter Four

Teetering at the edge of a black abyss, Angel fought to maintain consciousness. She forced herself to inhale a deep breath, released it slowly and felt her dizziness recede.

"The police wouldn't be looking for me if I hadn't killed him, would they?" she asked shakily, hoping Jordan would contradict her.

The forbidding set of his handsome features mirrored her distress, and she could almost hear the gears of his mind shifting rapidly behind the midnight-blue of his eyes.

When he spoke, caution tempered his voice. "Next of kin are always suspects in any murder case, because most victims are killed by someone they know."

Bile rose in her throat, and she swallowed convulsively to keep from being sick. How could she have murdered her ex-husband when the idea of killing anyone was so repugnant?

She is believed to be traveling with her two-year-old daughter, Brittany.... The words from the newscast rang in her head, precipitating another sickening wave of nausea and light-headedness.

Struggling against the blackness, she drew a deep breath. "If Brittany isn't with me, where is she?"

Jordan sat beside her and clutched her shoulders. "Don't go to pieces on me now, Angel."

"My name is Sara," she said flatly.

"You'll always be Angel to me. And the nickname's a good cover."

She met his rock-steady gaze and fought against panic. "Is it possible I've lost my mind? That I killed my husband, even my—"

"Stop it!" He gave her a shake, then gathered her into his arms. "You're exhausted and suffering from a blow to the head, but you're *not* crazy."

When she'd awakened this morning without memories, she had believed her situation as bad as it could get, but lack of memory was a stroll in the park compared to the crisis she faced now.

She yielded instinctively to the comfort of Jordan's embrace. Rocking her gently against his chest, he smoothed her hair with a gentle hand. Her silent tears drenched his shirt where her cheek rested against the reassuring thud of his heart. Jordan was the anchor that grounded her against the unknowns she faced, the rock of assurance that kept her from shattering into a million hysterical pieces.

Terrifying, yet unanswerable, questions battered her. If she *had* murdered her ex-husband and worse, she would never be able to live with that knowledge.

And if she *hadn't,* without her memory, how could she clear her name and find her daughter?

"What should I do?" Her voice cracked with emotion.

He tightened his arms around her. "You should get some sleep. You can't do anything tonight. And who knows? You could awake tomorrow with your memory intact."

If she *had* killed David Swinburn, she didn't want to remember. She shivered at the possibility that her mind had shut down to save her from recalling that awful deed.

Jordan released her, knelt beside the bed and, as if she were a child, removed her shoes and socks. The tenderness of his gesture and the comforting contact of his hands with her bare feet bolstered her courage.

"Do *you* think I killed David Swinburn?"

He stood and turned to rummage in the bag he'd carried in with the cooler. When he faced her again with his features composed, his expression told her nothing about his feelings.

"A good detective keeps an open mind until all the evidence is in."

"Are you a good detective?"

A flash of sorrow destroyed the neutrality of his face. "I was, in the beginning."

Abruptly, in the quiet coziness of the motel room, a barrier had dropped between them, as invisible as air, as impenetrable as steel.

With cool politeness, he offered the clothing he'd

removed from his bag. "If you don't want to sleep in your clothes, you can wear this."

Afraid to trust her voice, she accepted his T-shirt without thanks. As if walking through a thick fog of unreality, she went into the bathroom to change. Fearful of what she might discover in her eyes, she avoided the mirror and stripped off jeans, sweatshirt and bra and shrugged into the soft, oversize shirt that dipped to her thighs.

A sudden weariness clobbered her like a knockout punch, bringing with it blessed numbness. Leaving her discarded clothes in a heap, she stumbled into the bedroom to the far side of the king-size bed, where Jordan had turned back the covers, and slipped between the cool sheets.

The sleep of exhaustion closed in and erased the horror of the day the instant she hit the pillow. As she lost consciousness, she decided Jordan's tucking a blanket around her with a soft good-night must have been a dream.

AT SUNRISE, JORDAN SIPPED complimentary motel coffee from a foam cup and dangled his feet from the seawall outside the room. Along the tide line, seagulls scavenged for food in the pale light and split the dawn quiet with their strident cries. The bracing smell of salt water and the cloying sweetness of oleanders in bloom filled the air.

A typical, peaceful morning on the Gulf Coast. At least, it should have been, but Angel's sudden and problematic intrusion into his life had blown his formerly calm existence to hell and back.

Had she killed David Swinburn?

Gentle and vulnerable, she seemed an unlikely murderer. His too-brief police career had taught him, however, that, contrary to movie and television plots, most killers weren't calculating and evil, but regular folks who yielded to their baser instincts in a moment of passionate rage. And a spouse was always a suspect because of the thin line between love and hate and the vehement fervor those emotions generated.

He picked up a smooth shell and skipped it along the surface of the bay, disturbing the water's calm just as Angel had ruffled his life. He had learned long ago that apathy, not hate, was the opposite of love. And he'd never heard of anyone committing murder while caught in the throes of apathy.

He had to consider the possibility that Angel, provoked by something her ex-husband had said or done, had lost control, killed him and fled in horror at her actions.

If she *was* a killer, what was he going to do about it? He had returned to the dilemma he had wrestled with all night, a ticklish situation that placed his conscience at odds with his professional training.

If he were smart, he would hand her over to the police and let them sort it out. But how could he just dump her when she had no memories, nothing to use in her own defense?

As an experienced investigator, he'd cleared his share of cases, and he still had his skills. He could hide Angel until he'd uncovered the facts of the case or until her memories returned. He shrugged off that option, too, knowing if the police—or the thugs on her trail—found her in the meantime, he didn't want to be responsible for the consequences.

He had only one other choice and had leaned toward that solution all night. It looked about as appealing in the morning light as it had then. The lesser of three evils.

It was time to act.

He set aside his empty cup and pulled his phone from the pocket of his shorts. The eight rings it took Michael Winslow to answer and the grogginess in his voice indicated he'd probably been asleep.

"Mike, Jordan Trouble. I need your help."

"What's up?" An alert, all-business tone replaced Michael's grogginess.

"I'm on my cell phone, so I'd rather not say. You never know who's monitoring the airways. Can you meet me?"

"Just tell me when and where."

"How about where the softball team meets after practice? In an hour?"

"See you then."

Jordan hoisted himself to his feet and pocketed his phone. Placing the call had been the easy part. The tough part would be telling Angel what he'd done.

After a last, longing look at the bay and the channel that led to the open waters of the gulf, away from the monumental dilemma he'd stumbled into, he returned to the room, unlocked the door and slipped inside. Enough light seeped around the closed draperies to reveal Angel, curled on her side, asleep as he had left her.

The sight of her, her face flushed with sleep, one slender leg escaped from beneath the covers, sent a hot rush of desire straight to his groin. As if debating her problem all night hadn't been tough enough, he'd also had to resist the temptation to slide across the wide bed and pull her warm and supple body into his arms. Along with the lust, feelings he'd tried to bury washed over him, stirring his hunger for closeness. He had alienated himself from everyone who had ever loved him, and until last night he had welcomed the solitude.

A year ago, he'd learned the hard way that closeness brought its own kind of pain, and he refused to suffer that agony again. But most important of all, Angel already had the deck stacked against her. She didn't need his lack of detachment and subsequent bungling to add to her difficulties.

In another hour, she would be safe in Michael Winslow's capable hands, and as soon as the boat was ready, he'd take off for Key West, do a little scuba diving, fish for marlin and make *Oblivion* live up to her name.

Angel stirred and moaned in her sleep, and her plaintive whimper wrenched his heart.

Aw, damn.

Handing her over to Michael then turning his back wasn't going to be easy. The instant she'd walked into Mary Tiger's, she'd snagged him with those big brown eyes and lighted a fire among the cold ashes, all that remained of his heart. The prospect of her in his bed had its charm, but not for the long haul. She deserved better.

For a year now, he'd battled his demons alone—with some help from Mary Tiger. Keeping to himself was the only way he'd managed to stay sane and hold anger and grief at bay. He couldn't risk Angel's teaching him to care again. Leaving her with Michael would be doing himself—and her—a favor.

He leaned across the bed and jostled her soft, rounded shoulder. "Angel, wake up."

She stretched languorously with a wide, sleepy smile that stirred his senses and evoked a responding grin. But as consciousness claimed her, horror flooded the depths of her eyes, and her smile vanished. "The newscast—it wasn't just a bad dream?"

He shook his head. "Hurry and dress. We have to meet someone."

Her feathery eyebrows peaked with suspicion. "Who?"

"Michael Winslow."

Her look of mistrust turned to fear. "A cop?"

"A defense attorney."

She bolted upright, and the movement drew the thin cotton T-shirt taut across her high, firm breasts. He glanced away to squelch the warmth rising in his blood and avoid the accusation in her eyes.

"You're turning me in?" Her simple question hung heavy in the charged atmosphere of the room.

"No." He forced himself to face her, to watch disappointment flood her features. "You are."

"I can't."

"You don't have much choice—"

"How can I defend myself if I can't remember? And even worse—" She snapped off the words with trembling lips.

"What's even worse?"

"What if I'm guilty?" The agony in her hushed voice rebuked him for a traitor.

"Are you?"

"I don't know. I don't *feel* like a murderer, but how's a murderer supposed to feel?"

At the gloomy confusion in her eyes, he shoved his hands in his pockets to keep from holding her, consoling her. She needed competent legal advice, not solace from a guy whose own life was a mess.

"Let's take an objective look at your situation," he said more calmly than he felt. "Every cop in the state is on the lookout for you. You have two guys with bad intentions on your tail. And you have no idea where your daughter is. Is your memory any better today?"

She shook her head.

"If you turn yourself in, you'll be safe in jail from the men who're after you, and the police can turn their efforts to finding Brittany."

In defiance, she raised her chin a notch and crossed her arms over her breasts, but not before he noticed the trembling in her hands. "Can't I just stay in disguise and *you* help me find Brittany?"

"Believe me, things will go better for you if you surrender of your own free will. For me, too."

She lifted her head and confronted him with hurt in her eyes. "You're that anxious to get rid of me?"

Lucky for him, she had no idea how torn he was over his decision. She'd be better off with Michael than a washed-up ex-cop with no future. "If I stay with you, we could both end up in jail." A little guilt might nudge her in the right direction.

"Why would they arrest you? *You* haven't done anything."

"Except harboring a fugitive—" he ticked off the charges on his fingers "—obstruction of justice, possibly even accessory after the fact. Heard enough?"

She nodded, downcast. "Who is this Michael?"

"Winslow's a friend of mine, and one of the best criminal attorneys in the country."

"Can I trust him?"

"That's for you to decide, but if we're going to meet him, we have to hurry."

Varied emotions flitted across her face as she deliberated, until, finally, a mask of grim resolution settled over her. "I'll listen to what he has to say, but I'm not making any promises."

Uncurling her longs legs from the covers, she tugged the T-shirt modestly over her hips and hurried into the bathroom to dress.

JORDAN SCANNED THE WIDE alley on which Tom O'Riley, a retired sergeant from the Sunset Bay department, had built his sports bar. At the far end, rush-hour traffic thundered by on the boulevard, but none of the businesses on the alley itself had opened yet. A stray cat, prowling for scraps by the Dumpster across the way, was the only sign of life.

As if to keep from snatching the itchy hat and black wig from her head, Angel sat on her hands on the steps of the bar. Dark glasses covered her eyes, but the tense set of her jaw and shoulders transmitted her anxiety. She stiffened as a sleek, silver Infiniti turned into the alley and pulled to a stop beside them.

The tinted window on the driver's side slid down with an electronic purr. Michael Winslow, the top button of his oxford dress shirt undone, his red, patterned-silk tie loosened and long sleeves rolled above his wrists, greeted them with his jury-charming smile.

"Hop in. We can talk at my office over breakfast."

As if having second thoughts, Angel hung back until Jordan cupped her elbow and urged her forward. "It's okay. You have to trust me."

Unable to imagine what she must be feeling without memories or a familiar face to rely on, he opened the back door of Michael's car, then climbed in behind her.

Michael swiveled, introduced himself and reached over the seat to extend his hand.

"I'm…Angel." She shook his hand quickly, then clasped her own in her lap.

Michael cocked a questioning eyebrow, but Jordan shook his head, indicating explanations could wait.

His friend turned back to the wheel and drove out of the alley onto the traffic-choked boulevard.

Ten years earlier when he was a rookie cop, Jordan had met Michael, a wet-behind-the-ears assistant state attorney, on the ball field. Opposing players on their departments' softball teams, they'd often stayed late after games, consuming draft beer, pizza and endless hours of the ESPN cable network at their favorite watering hole.

The two could have been brothers, both tall and well-muscled with thick, light brown hair. But where Jordan's eyes were dark blue, Michael's were a deep ivy-green, and a spate of freckles across the bridge of his nose created an illusion of youthful innocence, a quality that served him well in the courtroom, especially with female jurors.

Both loners who excelled at their jobs, between their crime-fighting work and love of sports, they had found a lot in common. A few years later, when Jordan was promoted to detective, they had worked together on several important cases. Three years ago, Michael left the state attorney's office and opened his own practice, and Jordan had kept in touch, meeting his old friend often at Tom O'Riley's.

Until last April, when Jordan had lost contact with everyone.

He thrust the grim memories away. They were water under the bridge, and he had to concentrate on helping Angel—and not repeating his mistakes.

He flinched when she grabbed his arm, dug her

nails into his flesh and hissed between clenched teeth. "You promised. No police."

Following her terrified gaze, he saw that the car was approaching the modern glass-and-steel structure of the mainland headquarters of the Sunset Bay Police Department.

"Relax. Michael's office is only two blocks from here," he assured her.

When the Infiniti passed the imposing building without slowing, she reclined against the butter-soft leather seat and released her death grip on his forearm.

Michael turned the car onto a street lined with royal palms and restored Art Deco buildings. They traveled another block to a gleaming white building trimmed with bright turquoise, where he pulled into a narrow driveway. In a covered carport in a parking lot at the rear, he turned off the engine.

Jordan exited and scanned the empty lot before circling to open Angel's door. Without a word, she accompanied him, following Michael across the pavement, shaded from the hot morning sun by jacarandas thick with purple blossoms. Dense hedges of podocarpous concealed them from any onlookers in buildings on either side.

They stepped inside a rear entrance to a broad, air-conditioned hallway with a floor of Italian tiles and soothing white plaster walls hung with vivid modern art. Jordan suppressed a whistle at the elegance. Michael had come a long way from his cramped, utilitarian cubicle at the state attorney's office.

"The conference room is the second door on your left," Michael said. "We can talk there."

"May I use your rest room first?" A white line edged Angel's tight mouth, and for a moment, Jordan feared she was going to be sick.

"Sure. Meet us in the conference room."

Michael indicated a door on the right, and Angel lunged through it. Jordan followed Michael into the conference room, where Claire Sedgwick, Michael's rosy-cheeked, gray-haired secretary, was setting out a continental breakfast on the sideboard.

"Hold all my calls and appointments until we're finished here," Michael instructed her.

She nodded and left the room, passing Angel, on her way in.

Jordan watched Michael's jaw drop when he looked at Angel. She had removed her wig and hat in the rest room, and her blond hair framed her face like a sunlit cloud.

As if aware of Jordan's scrutiny, Michael quickly recovered the poker face he utilized so effectively in the courtroom. "Help yourselves to breakfast. Then we can talk."

Angel poured a cup of black coffee and selected a cranberry muffin before taking an upholstered seat at the massive mahogany table. Despite having little appetite, Jordan filled his plate and sat across from her.

Michael settled at the head of the table between them. "Now, Mrs. Swinburn, why don't you tell me everything?"

Jerking at his use of her name, Angel sloshed coffee onto the polished tabletop. "You recognize me?"

"Hard not to," Michael said with a congenial smile.

He grabbed a linen napkin from the sideboard and mopped up the spill before opening a second napkin and spreading it across the lap of his expensive trousers. "Especially since we've worked together for the last two years on the fund-raising committee for Sunset County's children's hospital. Don't you remember?"

"That's the problem," Jordan said, "or at least part of it. She doesn't remember *anything*."

"Holy—" Michael stifled the curse by downing a swallow of orange juice. "I've seen the news reports. You'd better tell me what you can of your side of the story."

Angel nodded to Jordan. "You first. Your memories go back further than mine."

"It started Sunday night," Jordan explained, "when Angel showed up at Mary Tiger's bar on the beach."

He described his scuffle with the men who had tried to kidnap her, her subsequent injury and carrying Angel to his boat. Then Angel, nervously crumbling her muffin, recounted the rest.

When she reached the end of her story, she added, "Jordan thinks I should turn myself in."

"He's right," Michael agreed.

"But I'm innocent...I have to be." Desperation edged her voice, but she held her composure.

Michael lowered his coffee cup and looked straight into her eyes. "All the more reason to turn yourself in and get to the bottom of this."

"But the police believe I killed him."

"As long as they're convinced you did it," Jordan said, "the cops won't be looking for anyone else. You can't convince them of your innocence unless you can refute their evidence. And they won't share that evidence until your attorney requests it."

The trust in her eyes stabbed him with fresh guilt over his plans to leave. He'd seen that trusting look before in other eyes, eyes that would never see anything again.

To avoid her gaze, he turned to Michael. "Several aspects of Angel's case don't make sense."

"Let's hear them." Michael leaned forward, giving Jordan his full attention, just as he had to Angel, his finely-tuned intelligence evident in the intensity of his green eyes.

"Mary Tiger said Angel—" Jordan stumbled at Michael's raised eyebrow "—uh, Sara was looking for me right before the scuffle when she lost her memory. It doesn't make sense that someone who's just killed her husband would wander into a public place in search of an ex-cop."

"You're right," Michael said.

Jordan glanced at Angel. "Then there's the break-in at her in-laws' house on Turtle Key. She went there almost immediately after David died. Why?"

"Could be she was angry and intended to kill them, too," Michael suggested. At Angel's horrified gasp, he held up his hands. "I'm only playing devil's advocate."

"The Swinburns were at home asleep," Jordan said. "If Angel had wanted to harm them, she could have, easily. No, I think she was searching for something."

"Brittany?" Michael suggested.

"Maybe. Or she was looking for a place to hide from the men who are after her."

"But *why* are they after me?" Angel's voice rose with frustration. "*None* of this makes sense."

"You'll know more after you turn yourself in," Jordan answered. "The state attorney's office will have to share all their evidence against you with Michael. Once you know what that evidence is, you can fit the pieces of the puzzle together."

The cop in him itched to get his hands on that evidence, but studying the case against her would only draw him in deeper and make leaving that much harder.

Across the burnished surface of the table, Angel leaned toward him, soft lips gently parted, flawless skin flushed and eyes bright with hope, radiating an innocence that couldn't be faked. If hers was the face of a killer, he'd lost his touch in assessing a suspect—or else his judgment had been compromised by other emotions.

He resisted becoming more entangled in Angel's problem—or the snare of her attraction. Time for him to bow out, and he was ready with the perfect excuse.

"Michael's brother Ryan does investigations for

him,'' Jordan explained to Angel, before looking to Michael. "Ryan can handle the detective work on Angel's case.''

"Ryan's in Tallahassee on another matter. He could be gone for weeks." Michael continued scribbling notes on a legal pad with a gold-and-ebony Mont Blanc pen.

The sense of inevitability that had gripped Jordan since his first encounter with Angel settled on him like a steel trap. The harder he fought responsibility for her, the tighter her hold on him grew.

She leaned toward Michael. "If I surrender to the police, will you represent me?''

"Yes.''

Michael picked up a phone from the credenza behind him and punched the intercom. "Claire, get Dr. Stuart Rosenbaum on the phone.''

"Rosenbaum?" Jordan said. "The psychiatrist?''

"I want Sara's amnesia evaluated before she surrenders to the police.''

Hurt filled Angel's eyes. "Don't you believe me?''

Michael placed his hand over hers. "What's important is whether the judge believes you've lost your memory or suspects you're playing for sympathy. I want a professional opinion the judge will respect *before* we attend the advisory hearing. Rosenbaum's the best there is.''

Jordan saw Michael's hand on Angel's, heard the soft consolation in the attorney's voice and watched her hang on his every word. An uncomfortable feeling shot through him, so foreign he needed a moment to identify it.

Jealousy.

With an inward groan, he slid deeper in his chair. He couldn't remember the green-eyed monster nipping him before. His plan to abandon her to Michael was looking less likely by the minute.

AT FOUR O'CLOCK that afternoon, Angel sat stiffly behind the defense table in the Circuit Court of Sunset County, her hands clasped in her lap. She issued up a silent prayer of gratitude that she'd been spared the indignity of handcuffs and leg irons at this hastily arranged advisory hearing.

She was thankful, too, she'd been allowed to dress in the conservative beige suit, ecru silk blouse and low heels Jordan had spirited from her apartment, instead of the shapeless orange coverall of a Sunset County inmate. The familiar fit of the clothes boosted her self-confidence.

Michael had pulled a few more strings and arranged for her advisory hearing in the courthouse, rather than the usual closed-circuit appearance with other prisoners, televised from the county jail.

But her deepest gratitude came from the fact that the authorities, realizing Brittany wasn't with her, had stepped up a statewide search for her daughter. She closed her eyes and prayed that Brittany, the daughter she couldn't remember, would be found safe—and soon.

At the table beside her, Michael rustled papers,

and behind the railing, Jordan sat with Dr. Rosenbaum, both ready, if called on, to testify to her amnesia. Jordan's steady and comforting gaze warmed her back.

Butterflies danced in her stomach, and her palms were damp, but her present nervousness was nothing compared to the stark terror she'd suffered when Jordan and Michael had accompanied her to the police station to turn herself in.

To avoid cameras and reporters, she'd been rushed into the police building through the sally port and had also exited there into the closed van that had brought her to the courthouse.

"All rise."

At the clerk's command, Michael's hand beneath her elbow propelled her to her feet. She managed to trade glances with Jordan and catch his nod of reassurance before Judge Wilbur Zacharias swooped onto the bench in a flapping black robe. He took his seat and peered at her over narrow bifocals.

"Sara Swinburn," he intoned in a booming voice consistent with the magnitude of his office, "you arc charged with murder in the first degree. How do you plead?"

Her mouth turned dry, and the unsteadiness in her knees made her appreciate Michael's supporting hand beneath her elbow.

She forced her response through stiff lips. "Not guilty, your honor."

The judge waved them into their chairs and addressed Michael. "Now, Mr. Winslow, I'm ready to hear your reasons why this hearing has deviated from every regular procedure in this county. And, believe me, they had better be good."

Chapter Five

Michael rose and straightened his double-breasted jacket with a purposeful movement that caught every gaze in the courtroom. Except Jordan's. He couldn't tear his attention from the dejected slope of Angel's shoulders.

Angel. He'd never be able to think of her as Sara.

Zacharias, dubbed Old Blood and Thunder by the legal community, had intentionally bullied her with his infamous fire-breathing speech and hawklike stare. Jordan scooted forward in his chair and leaned across the bar to warn her of the judge's notorious maneuvers.

"Relax," he whispered in her left ear, "Zacharias isn't as tough as he acts."

The subtle fragrance of her perfume, a honeysuckle scent that conjured up soft breezes, summer nights and an enticing picture of Angel in his arms teased his nose. He wondered if she'd ever enjoy the freedom of a summer night again, and the thought tied a cold, hard knot in his stomach.

Earlier he had located her apartment through the

phone company's directory assistance and gone there to collect her clothes for the hearing. Choosing the delicate crystal perfume bottle from her bedroom dresser, he had hoped the familiar fragrance would trigger her recollections, but the scent apparently hadn't helped. All her memories remained locked away.

While she had met with Dr. Rosenbaum, Jordan had selected her clothing according to Michael's instructions—simple and understated in neutral colors. Choosing the suit and blouse had been the easy part. Picking through lacy undergarments and silky stockings as insubstantial as a cloud had been an intimate and erotic experience, an act a man usually performed only for a lover or a wife.

Equally unsettling had been his futile search for clues to help in her defense. He had come away empty-handed, haunted by the poignant emptiness of little Brittany's sunny bedroom.

He forced his attention back to the proceedings when Michael stepped forward to address the judge.

"The circumstances of this case are extraordinary, your honor. The defendant suffers from amnesia and is unable to participate in her own defense. I have an expert who will testify her amnesia was induced by psychological trauma, and that incarceration will only exacerbate her condition."

Judge Zacharias raised bushy eyebrows, lifted a long, bony finger and pointed at the attorney accusingly. "Are you suggesting, Counselor, that I release

Ms. Swinburn simply because she finds our accommodations stressful?''

Jordan empathized with Angel's cringe at the sarcasm in the judge's voice, but Michael, familiar with Zacharias's methods, didn't blink.

''Not entirely. The sooner she regains her memory, the sooner she will be fit for trial. Without the stress of jail and with the able help of Dr. Rosenbaum, she hopes to overcome her amnesia quickly.'' He paused, waiting for Zacharias's reaction.

''Is that all?'' the judge asked.

''There is another issue at stake besides the murder of David Swinburn.''

''Please—'' Zacharias waved his hand, causing the sleeve of his robe to flutter like a giant wing ''—enlighten me.''

''Ms. Swinburn's two-year-old daughter is missing. The police believe if Ms. Swinburn can regain her memory, she can help locate her daughter.''

Zacharias propped his elbows on the bench, steepled his fingers and scrutinized Angel over the tops of his bifocals. Jordan's reluctant admiration grew when she straightened in her chair and met the judge's gaze unflinchingly.

''Very well, Counselor. Call your first witness.''

''Jordan Trouble, former detective-lieutenant with the Sunset Bay Police Department.''

Jordan rose, proceeded through the gate to the witness stand and raised his hand to be sworn in by the clerk.

When he took his seat, Zacharias leaned toward him, compassion gleaming in his dark eyes.

"Happy to see you're still among the living, Lieutenant Trouble," he muttered in a low voice.

"Thank you, your honor."

The knot in Jordan's stomach started to unravel. Zacharias hadn't changed. A kind heart still beat beneath that crusty exterior. Michael's plan for Angel's release might work after all.

In concise, simple terms, Jordan described meeting Angel and her subsequent amnesia. Her gaze never left his face during the telling, and he stared at Michael to avoid the distraction of her luminous eyes.

When Jordan finished his testimony, Dr. Rosenbaum took the stand and presented his diagnosis that her amnesia had been induced by emotional trauma.

Rosenbaum stepped down and exited the courtroom, and Michael again addressed the judge. "Given the circumstances of Ms. Swinburn's amnesia, which renders her incapable of participating in her own defense, I ask that the court set bail, so that she is spared further anxiety by incarceration and can receive treatment, including stimulation of her memory by familiar surroundings."

Zacharias scowled. "Bail in a capital case is highly unusual."

"I agree, your honor, but the circumstances of this case are also unusual. And there's Ms. Swinburn's missing daughter to consider."

"We'll take a short recess while I consider my

decision." The judge rapped his gavel and left the bench in a rustle of black fabric.

Michael returned to Angel at the defense table, and Jordan joined them.

"There's a soda machine down the hall," the attorney said. "Sit tight and I'll bring you something to drink."

He strode up the aisle toward the exit, and Jordan sat beside Angel. "How are you holding up?"

She shrugged, outwardly nonchalant, but a white line of apprehension edged her lips, colored now with a subtle coral lipstick that suited her quiet elegance better than Reckless Red. "I'm numb. None of this seems real."

"It's almost over."

She clasped her hands on the tabletop until her knuckles went white and rubbed one thumb over the other. "Looks like I'm headed to jail."

"Zacharias could grant bail."

"What good would that do? I don't have any money. The balance in the checkbook you brought from my apartment shows I'm almost broke."

She wasn't exaggerating. After she had written Michael a modest check for his retainer, her funds had been pitifully small.

"We'll find a bail bonds agent to guarantee your bail."

"Just like that? Don't they need some kind of collateral, in case I skip the country?"

"The collateral doesn't have to cover the entire bail. You can use real estate—"

"The lease you found says my apartment's rented."

"—or a car."

She shook her head. "I don't know where my car is. Neither do the police."

He cradled her clenched hands and gently kneaded the tightness from them. "Zacharias could set bail so low, you might not need collateral."

Fifteen minutes later, back in his seat behind the bar, Jordan was less confident when the judge returned to the courtroom to announce his decision.

The ruling would be a tough call. Bail was almost never granted in capital cases. Because Florida law allowed the death penalty for first-degree murder, a judge had to consider that the accused might flee prosecution rather than risk execution in Old Sparky, the state's infamous electric chair.

The soda Jordan had drunk during the break ate at his insides, and anxiety congested his throat. The idea of Angel sentenced to die in Old Sparky had made his heart ache and initiated his queasy stomach.

But maybe events wouldn't come to that. Angel's circumstances were unique. If Zacharias refused to grant bail, the media would rip him to shreds over his harsh treatment of a mother who couldn't remember and his apparent disdain for her missing child.

The judge, his gloomy expression grimmer than usual, climbed to his seat. Crossing his arms on the bench, he bent toward Michael with the mournful look of a kid who'd lost his dog. His refusal to look at Angel sent a chill through Jordan, and he had to hold himself back from reaching out to reassure her.

"You've presented me with an interesting dilemma, Counselor." The judge's bleak voice echoed in the almost empty room. "To grant bail in a capital case would set a dangerous precedent."

Michael remained silent, and everyone in the room, from the bailiff to Angel and a handful of spectators, seemed to hold their breath.

"But I'm not a heartless man," Zacharias continued with a smile that didn't reach his eyes. "I recognize that Ms. Swinburn cannot participate in her defense without her memory, and I feel for the loss of her little girl. I have a granddaughter that age."

Jordan's hope rekindled. Maybe Zacharias *was* going to grant bail.

"However—" with one word, the judge dashed his expectations "—I have a responsibility to this community. I can't just turn an accused murderer loose. She must be remanded to the custody of someone who can assure she is no threat to the people of this state."

In a flash of precognition, Jordan felt the noose of inevitability cinch a notch tighter.

"Therefore, I set bail at seven hundred and fifty thousand dollars and remand Sara Swinburn to the custody of former Detective-Lieutenant Jordan Trouble, who will guarantee that she receive therapy for her amnesia and be responsible for her conduct until she returns for trial, the date of which will be set at an arraignment hearing three weeks from today."

Zacharias banged the gavel, rose and, without another glance at Angel, disappeared into his chambers.

Jordan sat in stunned silence.

Michael twisted in his chair and spoke to him across the bar. "We won. Why do I feel like we lost?"

Jordan shook his head in disbelief. "The old fox is playing both ends against the middle. Because he set bail, he can't be accused of being unsympathetic to a mother with amnesia and a missing daughter."

Michael grimaced. "But he set it so high, there's little likelihood Sara can make it. Essentially he's assured that she'll remain behind bars."

The bailiff moved forward to claim his prisoner, and Jordan recognized Biff Langdon, a veteran police officer who'd turned bailiff when his knee went bad.

"Give us a couple minutes, will you, Biff?"

Biff nodded and moved away.

Angel's face had lost its color, but she stood with her shoulders back, head high. Her gaze met Jordan's, but without reproach. He blamed himself enough for both of them. If he hadn't encouraged her to surrender to police, she'd still be free.

Only a slight tremor in her full bottom lip belied her poise.

"I'm sorry." Michael placed his hand on her shoulder. "I—"

"Ahem."

Jordan turned at the sound of a throat clearing behind them.

A short, balding man in gray slacks and a pink

sport shirt pulled tight over a rounded paunch hovered in the aisle. He thrust a soiled business card toward Michael. ''Joe Spacek. Maybe I can help.''

Jordan remembered Spacek as a bail bonds agent who had guaranteed bail for some of the worst slime to pass through the courts of Sunset County. He was alleged to have mob connections and obviously had some tie-in to the police department, since even the media hadn't known about Angel's advisory hearing. Spacek's presence raised nagging questions about how he had obtained his information.

''What are you doing here?'' Jordan asked. ''Nobody knew about this hearing.''

Spacek shuffled his feet. ''I had a matter to attend to in the courthouse and noticed this room was in use. Figured I'd drum up some business.''

Jordan didn't believe him. ''Not even you would risk posting a three-quarter-million bond.''

Angel glanced sharply from Jordan to Spacek. ''It's no risk. I don't intend to run away.''

''That's not the point.'' Michael's expression reflected Jordan's distrust. ''Spacek needs big collateral to insure that much money.''

Joe shook his bald head, and late afternoon sunlight slanting in the tall windows glinted off his oily scalp. ''Not necessarily. I can tell Mrs. Swinburn is a class act. I got no worries about her not showing up for trial.''

Jordan appraised Spacek with skepticism. ''When did you get to be such a trusting humanitarian?''

''Hey.'' He shrugged his meaty shoulders and offered his card again. "I ain't pretending the publicity on this won't be good for business."

Spacek was lying through his yellow teeth. With his connections, he didn't need advertising. Jordan met Michael's gaze. "What do you think?"

This time Michael grabbed Spacek's card before he could withdraw it again. "Never look a gift horse in the mouth."

THAT EVENING, ANGEL STOOD with Jordan in the apartment where the police said she'd lived for the past year and a half. Nothing seemed familiar, neither the restful blue-and-green color scheme of the living room, the all-white bedroom with its curtains, bedspread and pillows edged in Battenburg lace, or the cozy kitchen with cabinets of bleached oak.

None of the clothing she'd packed in suitcases for Michael to deliver to Jordan's boat in dry dock had brought back any memories. Neither could she explain the overwhelming sense of satisfaction the strange garments with which she'd filled the bags had given her.

After posting her bail through Joe Spacek, Michael had whisked Jordan and her away in his luxurious car and driven north to St. Petersburg and an early dinner in a quaint, exclusive restaurant off Beach Drive, where the maître'd had greeted Michael by name.

Still shaky from her encounters with the Sunset Bay police and the irascible Judge Zacharias, she had remained quiet and eaten little. What little appetite she'd had disappeared entirely at her companions' conversation over their entrées.

"It doesn't make sense," Michael insisted. "Spacek's a businessman. Unprincipled and disgusting, but still a businessman. Why would he risk three-quarters of a million dollars?"

Jordan grinned with the appealing charm she remembered from their first meeting, and she welcomed its return. Neither of them had found much to smile about in the last twenty-four hours.

"Since the judge remanded Angel to *my* custody, maybe Spacek's putting his money on my sterling reputation," Jordan said, "knowing I'll make certain she shows up for trial."

"It's possible," Michael said thoughtfully.

Jordan's grin faded. "But I don't think so. Spacek doesn't trust anybody, least of all a cop."

"If he isn't certain I'll appear for trial, why was he willing to post such a huge bond?" Angel asked.

Jordan's blue eyes were hard with anger. "Because Spacek doesn't really care whether you keep your court date."

"You think somebody's providing Spacek's collateral for Sara?" Michael asked.

Jordan nodded grimly "Somebody who doesn't want Angel in jail. Could be the same person who paid those two thugs who tried to grab her in Mary Tiger's."

"Whoever it is," Michael said thoughtfully, "has to have big bucks to guarantee that large a sum."

Jordan tossed his peach-colored napkin on the table in frustration. "That certainly narrows the field. Sunset County has the highest median income in the state. We'll need more than wealth to identify a suspect."

Their deductions frightened her. "Isn't it possible some anonymous friend arranged for my bail?"

Jordan exchanged an unreadable glance with Michael across the table before covering her hand with his. "Let's hope you're right. But if I'm to keep you safe, I have to consider the worst-case scenario and be prepared for it."

"What *is* the worst-case scenario?" she asked, not really wanting to know.

Michael frowned. "That whoever guaranteed your bail wants you out of jail where you're accessible."

"Accessible? Why?"

He shifted uneasily on the leather banquette, and his reluctance to answer sent a chill down her back. "You could have information this person needs—information he doesn't want you to share with anyone."

"Are you saying he wants me dead?" She had endured so much already, the idea of a hired killer coming after her brought no surprise. She braced herself for more fear, but all she felt was exhaustion.

"Don't worry," Michael said. "Jordan will protect you."

Jordan had squeezed her hand in encouragement, but doubt had flickered through his eyes.

Now, as he rummaged through her apartment for a second time that day, collecting names and addresses of anyone who might help his investigation, she wondered about the source of his uncertainty.

Michael obviously believed in Jordan's ability to safeguard her, but Jordan apparently wasn't convinced he could keep her from harm. Had he guessed who was after her and assessed her pursuer's strength and resources? Or did his doubt spring from shattered confidence? Perhaps the bullet that drove him off the police force had wounded more than his shoulder.

She shut her mind against more unanswered questions. Because of her lost memories, she knew Jordan Trouble better than anyone else on earth, and, ironically, she hardly understood him. The next three weeks, at any rate, should teach her a great deal about her rescuer. Thanks to Judge Zacharias, for the next twenty-one days, until the arraignment hearing, Jordan couldn't leave her side.

She took a last look around the bedroom and turned off the light. When she entered the living room, Jordan looked up from the desk he was searching. His tousled, sun-streaked hair tumbled across his high forehead, a devilish grin formed a deep dimple in his tanned cheek, and approval shone in the night-sky blue of his eyes.

She had already learned he was more than just a handsome face and sexy body. In spite of the uncertainty she'd witnessed earlier, she had no doubt he was a man she could rely on, a friend who would be there for her and a trained protector who would guard her with his life.

"I'm almost finished here," he said. "We can leave in a minute."

She crossed into Brittany's darkened bedroom, decorated with yellow-and-white gingham visible only by the single light from the living room. Of all the rooms in the apartment, this one evoked the most emotion, made her memories hover almost within reach.

In the white, spindled Jenny Lind crib, a well-worn white bear wearing a limp ribbon of yellow satin leaned against the pillow. She picked up the bear and held it in her arms. The familiar scent of baby powder filled her nose, inundating her with a longing so fierce, she gasped at the pain. Her knees buckled, and she sank into the white rocker with yellow gingham cushions beside the bed.

A tiny music box topped with figures of the polar bears Klondike and Snow from Sea World in Orlando—how had she remembered that?—sat on a low table beside her chair. She turned it over, wound the key and replaced it. The tinkling notes of "Teddy Bears' Picnic" filled the room, and she closed her eyes and rocked gently to the music.

She was standing in front of a wide expanse of glass that separated her from a frigid polar pool. A little girl in a denim OshKosh playsuit and tiny red sneakers wiggled in her arms, clapped her hands, still pudgy with baby fat, and shrieked a delighted laugh.

"*Wook, Mommy! Bay-uhs!* Big *bay-uhs.*"

Angel bolted from the chair and dashed into the living room. "I remember!"

Jordan, who had been tying the flap on an accordion file bulging with papers, dropped the bundle on the desk and hurried toward her.

Embarrassed at her outburst, she shook her head. "I remember Brittany. She's not just a photograph any longer." Tears blurred her vision. "I feel as if a part of me has been ripped away."

He encircled her with his strong arms and pulled her close. "We'll find her. Maybe you left her in someone's care. When we go back to the motel, we'll look through the papers I've collected and start calling your friends and family. Someone has to know where she is."

With the ache in her throat almost choking her, she rested her head on his shoulder and yielded to the consolation of his embrace. He had given her hope, and while it didn't banish her terrible yearning for her daughter, it eased her pain.

He stepped back and lifted her chin with his finger until her eyes met his. "We'll find her, Angel. I promise you."

With the back of his hand, he wiped the tears from her cheeks, then dipped his head and sealed his promise with a kiss. He tasted of sun and salt and sea, and she pressed against his firm body. Drowning in forgetfulness and pain, she clung to him, a lone rock of solidarity in her nebulous world without a past, and a living, breathing shield against her fears.

Abruptly, he released her. "Sorry."

She blinked in confusion. "Sorry?"

His eyes glowed almost black with passion, and he appeared as shaken as she was. "I took advantage of your grief. I had no right—"

She placed her fingers on his lips, hot and swollen from their kiss. "Please, don't say you're sorry again."

"I won't—" amusement sparkled in his eyes "—because it would be a lie. I'm not sorry I kissed you."

He had stirred her senses for the first time that she could remember, and he had bolstered her hope that they'd find her daughter. She returned his smile. "Neither am I."

"We'd better go."

She nodded. If they continued looking at each other much longer, she wouldn't be able to resist resuming where they'd left off, and she knew where that would lead. She had to concentrate on finding Brittany—and on not distracting Jordan from helping her.

He picked up the heavy file. "I've collected every name and phone number I could find. Maybe one of these people has Brittany." He hesitated. "There's just one thing that puzzles me."

"What's that?"

"My name isn't in here, so how did you learn about me and where to find me?"

She shook her head in frustration. "I don't know."

"*Why* were you looking for me?"

"Do you think my contacting you had something to do with David's murder?"

He studied her with bottomless blue eyes, eyes a woman could drown in if she wasn't careful. "You're the only one who can answer that question—" the familiar boyish grin that made her heart flutter split his face "—and so far, you're not talking."

"I remembered Brittany. Maybe the rest will come back to me soon."

He nodded. "Michael's office is only a few blocks from here. If we walk there, he can give us a lift to the motel. We don't want anyone tracing your whereabouts through a cab company."

He switched off the desk lamp, and low voices sounded outside the door in the front hall.

"I tell ya, this is a waste of time, Frank. She wouldn't be stupid enough to come back here when she knows we're looking for her."

"Shut up and pick the lock."

Angel surveyed the room in panic. The apartment had one entrance. Sliding glass doors in the living room led only to a small third-floor balcony.

Jordan grabbed her hand and whispered with his lips against her ear. "Come with me."

He tugged her toward the glass doors. She had no choice but to follow.

Behind her, the tumblers of the front-door lock clicked. Ahead was a three-story drop to the parking lot.

They were trapped.

Chapter Six

Jordan closed the sliding door behind them and pulled Angel toward a corner of the balcony filled by an overgrown ficus in a terra-cotta jardiniere.

"That won't hide us," she whispered.

"Not the tree." He swept aside branches. "Behind this door."

A utility closet was built into the balcony wall. He pushed her inside, pressed in behind her and closed the door, counting on the compact leaves of the ficus to conceal the entrance. Earlier, in the bright sunlight, when he searched the apartment the first time, he had almost missed the closet, whose entry had been camouflaged by the builder as part of the board-and-batten wall. With any luck, Angel's pursuers would overlook it entirely in the darkness.

A metallic rattle and Angel's muffled exclamation shattered the silence in the confined space.

"What's in here?" she whispered, so close he could feel her breath against his shoulder.

"An old barbecue grill, a tricycle—"

"Spiders?"

"Maybe."

She hurtled against him and latched her arms around his waist. "Roaches?"

"Probably."

Burying her face against his chest, she mumbled, "I *hate* bugs."

At her quiver of revulsion, he dropped the folder at his feet and, abandoning resistance, wrapped his arms around her, reveling in the perfect fit of their bodies. Despite the seductive pleasure of holding her, he forced himself to concentrate on sounds coming from the apartment.

"Believe me—" his lips moved against the silky strands of her hair "—bugs are the least of our worries."

As if to underscore his claim, a door banged against a wall inside, and she shuddered again.

"Not another word," he whispered, and flattened them both against the rear wall of the closet, as far from the door as possible.

His pulse thundered in his ears, and despite the layers of clothing between them, the frantic rhythm of her heart banged against his chest. He recalled the sweet, stimulating taste of her kiss and how he'd longed to lift her in his arms, carry her into the bedroom and make love to her among the nest of white pillows until they were both too tired to move.

Keep this up, and she'll wind up just like Jenny.

The thought doused his ardor as effectively as an icy shower. With a sinking sensation in his stomach, he reminded himself Angel was depending on him to keep her safe, and in order to guard her life, he couldn't lose his focus.

When he'd recognized the voices at the door, with an ingrained movement he couldn't seem to break, he'd reached for his gun at the back of his waist. If he'd had a weapon, he could have surprised the intruders at the door and held them until the police arrived.

Or I could have committed another fatal error.

He'd learned the hard way that a gun didn't guarantee success and had refused ever to rely on one again. His compact automatic, formerly his backup for his departmental gun, was locked in a bulkhead cabinet on his boat. On his next trip into deep waters, he intended to throw it overboard and, with luck, drown bad memories along with it.

The glass doors to the balcony slid open, and the wall behind him vibrated, setting his reflexes on alert. Footsteps thudded on the balcony floor. He had done a quick inventory of the closet's contents earlier. It contained nothing he could use effectively as a weapon. He'd be hard-pressed to ward off a gun-toting opponent with a Big Wheel.

"I told ya she wouldn't be here, Frank." The clarity of the hushed voice indicated the man was only inches from their hiding place. "If she was dumb enough to come back here, we woulda caught her by now."

"She's with that ex-cop, wherever she is."

Jordan connected the voice to the weasel-faced man from the bar.

"But where'd they go? His boat just disappeared. How do ya hide a forty-foot boat?"

"Now who's being stupid, Sidney? There're small marinas and private docks all over where Trouble could hide. And the man is shrewd. He knows we're looking for his boat, so my guess is he ditched it and headed for dry land."

"Okay, since you're so smart, where do we look now? It's a big state, and James is antsy. And when the boss gets antsy, *we* catch the flak."

"Search the apartment. Copy every name and address you find. She could be hiding with someone she knows."

"But Spacek told us she lost her memory. He said that's why the judge let her out."

"And you believe that?" Frank's derisive laugh carried clearly into the closet. "Claiming his client has amnesia is one of Winslow's legal-eagle tricks. He wanted to get her out of jail and throw us off her trail by making us think she can't remember."

"If she *can* remember, how come she ain't blabbed to the cops?"

"We don't know she hasn't. Quit your chattering and start searching for names. Use gloves and leave everything as you found it. We don't want to tip off anybody that we've been here."

In the dark, stuffy utility closet, Jordan, thankful he'd beaten them to the search, nudged the reassuring bulk of the accordion folder with his foot. His hunch had been right. Evidently, someone named James had provided Spacek the collateral to insure Angel's release, then set his hired thugs on her trail.

Jordan struggled to ignore the curves of her supple body pressed between him and the wall. If there was ever a time he shouldn't be preoccupied with Angel's undeniable magnetism, it was now.

Slamming doors, mutters and footfalls reverberated inside the apartment, marking the slow progress of Frank and Sidney's search. Sweat rolled down Jordan's forehead and into his eyes, but he couldn't risk moving to wipe it away. Angel's breathing grew raspy and shallow, and he feared one or both of them would pass out from lack of oxygen and the suffocating heat before Frank and Sidney left.

Finally, Frank's voice boomed from the living room near the open balcony door. "The only names and addresses in the whole place are in the damn phone book. She must have been here before us and cleared them out."

"Does that mean she really ain't lost her memory?"

"It means we have to find her fast. James wants her dead, but we can't kill her if we don't know where she is."

Angel stiffened, but Jordan didn't flinch. He had already guessed why the men were after her.

"We'll have to use her kid as bait," Sidney said.

Angel's quick intake of breath hissed in the silence.

"I like the way you think, Sidney. Let's get out of here." Frank's ruthless laughter filtered into the utility closet, and Jordan clamped his jaw against rising rage.

A few seconds later, the apartment's front door slammed. Angel stirred beneath him, but Jordan held her still, wanting to make certain both men had left. "Not yet. Stay here."

Groping carefully in the darkness to avoid disturbing the stored paraphernalia, he reached the door and opened it a crack. Fresh, cool air flowed in, and he inhaled deeply to clear the mugginess in his head. Night sounds of singing cicadas, a loud television on the floor below and a distant siren drifted on the breeze.

"Where to now?"

Sidney spoke, so loud and close that Jordan jumped, thinking the intruders had returned, before he realized the voice had risen from the parking lot below.

"We'll keep searching for Trouble," Frank said. "We find him, we find the woman."

Jordan waited until their car started before stepping onto the dark balcony. The departing vehicle was too far away to read the lighted license plate, and in the shadowy parking lot, he couldn't identify the make or color of the dark sedan.

He returned to the utility closet, scooped up the folder and gave Angel a hand as she threaded through the tangle of objects to the entrance.

Outside the closet, she bent forward with her hands on her thighs, sucking in fresh air like a winded runner.

"They have Brittany," she gasped.

"We don't know that for sure." He didn't add that if Frank and Sidney and their mysterious boss named James didn't have the little girl, they would definitely try to find her.

She shook her head. "I have to find Brittany before those two killers get to her. You heard what they said."

He nodded, but didn't have the heart to tell her just how tough finding Brittany might be.

A POD OF SLEEK DOLPHINS frolicked in the boat's wake the next morning as Jordan headed west, away from the rising sun. He'd had only a few hours' sleep, but he wanted to reach open water as soon as possible, just in case Frank and Sidney decided to check local marinas in search of his boat.

Leaving the Intracoastal Waterway, he allowed himself a self-satisfied smile. The thugs could search for *Oblivion* till hell froze over, but they wouldn't find her. Thanks to his friend at the marina dry dock, whose discretion he could count on, *Oblivion* had been transformed. Her formerly black trim now glistened as blue as the Florida sky, and a new name replaced the old one on her stern. Paying for the metamorphosis had maxed out his credit card, but he wouldn't worry about that until the bill arrived in thirty days.

More pressing concerns occupied him now. Like keeping Angel out of the hands of two hired killers and finding her little girl before they did. Last night, when he and Angel returned to Michael's office, the attorney had volunteered to give them a hand in their search. After they had filled Michael in on events in Angel's apartment, he flipped rapidly through the contents of the file Jordan had gathered.

"I'll turn these names and numbers over to Claire and her assistant first thing tomorrow," Michael said. "If we don't locate Brittany, we can at least narrow our search from the results of their phone calls."

"I'll help," Angel offered.

Jordan shook his head. "Not a good idea. Frank and Sidney know Michael's your attorney. They may stake out his office in case you show up."

"Jordan's right. You should stay out of sight."

"You mean do nothing while my baby's missing?" Spots of vivid color blotched her cheeks.

"I'll need your help," Jordan said in a placating tone, "interviewing the staff at David Swinburn's estate. They may know something about Brittany's whereabouts or who this James is. Besides, the last place Frank and Sidney will expect to find you is at the scene of the crime, so you should be safe there."

"Speaking of which," Michael said, "the house is off-limits until the crime scene unit is finished there."

"Maggie's orders?" Jordan asked.

"She runs a tight investigation," Michael said.

"Is Maggie the policewoman who interviewed me at the station?" Angel asked.

Jordan nodded. "Maggie Henderson is the best detective on the force."

"She moved into first place only after you resigned," Michael said.

Jordan shifted uncomfortably in the upholstered conference chair. Since his final interview with Internal Affairs, he had refused to talk with anyone about his former job or associates, and he wasn't about to break his silence now. "Are the grounds of the estate cordoned off, too?"

"Since you're my official investigator on this case, Maggie's granting you access to the grounds and outbuildings. You can interview the staff outdoors if you have to, but—" Michael glanced at Angel "—I suggest you keep out of sight as much as possible. With your looks, Sara, you draw a lot of attention, especially now that your picture's plastered on every TV screen and newspaper in the county."

Angel had taken Michael's warning to heart. Although it was almost midnight when he dropped them at the motel, she had marched into the bathroom with a resolute expression and the Wal-Mart bag in hand. A half hour later she emerged with her blond hair cropped in a bouncy cut just below her ears and dyed a honey-maple shade that matched her eyes.

Jordan had barely time to admire the results before she dropped into the deep sleep of exhaustion, still wearing the clothes she'd worn to court. She didn't rouse when he removed her shoes and tucked a blanket over her.

Exhausted, he set the alarm for five o'clock, lay beside her and fell instantly into a deep, restorative sleep, oblivious, for once, of temptation slumbering beside him.

When the alarm went off, they had both showered and dressed in casual clothes, then walked to the marina in the early morning darkness. The boat, complete with its new name and accent color, was tied at the pier beside the office, gassed up and ready to go. Late last night, Michael had loaded their clothes and supplies while it was still in dry dock.

"Heavenly Days?" Her eyebrows rose in surprise. "It's built exactly like your boat."

"It *is* my boat. Think Frank and Sidney will notice?"

"Where did you get the name?"

"It was my grandmother's favorite expression. I can hear her now. 'Heavenly days, Jordan, did you eat *all* the applesauce cookies I just baked?'"

"Lawman Jordan Trouble, a cookie thief? Who would have guessed?"

He welcomed her teasing. Lately, she hadn't had much to smile about. "There's a lot you don't know about me."

Her grin disappeared. "Until my memory returns, there's a lot I don't know about everything."

Her smile had faded too fast, and he tried to coax it back. "*Heavenly Days* is an appropriate name for a boat for an angel, don't you think?"

"Some angel." Her face twisted in an ironic grimace. "Out on bail for murder."

He placed his hands on her shoulders and looked her in the eyes. "We'll dig out the truth about what really happened to David Swinburn, and when we do, I have a feeling you'll be in the clear.''

She met his gaze without blinking. ''Clearing me of murder can wait. First, we have to find Brittany.''

He didn't know how she stood it, unable to remember, her daughter missing and a murder charge hanging over her head. If he had her problems, he'd need a padded room. The thought brought back memories of too many nights when he'd come close to needing that padded room himself, and out of nowhere, the hunger for a stiff drink ambushed him and the bottle of Absolut with the unbroken seal, stashed in the galley cabinet, beckoned him. Through the sheer force of willpower, he conquered his thirst. He couldn't protect Angel from killers if he was three sheets to the wind.

''We'll find Brittany,'' he assured her with more confidence than he felt. ''This morning Michael's staff will begin calling the names we found in your apartment. If Brittany is with one of your friends, we'll know soon.''

''And if she isn't?'' Her bearing remained determined, but her eyes conveyed her fear.

He refused to add to her alarm by voicing his misgivings. ''Then someone on Swinburn's staff might know where she is.''

''Wouldn't they have told the police already if they knew?''

He shrugged. ''Some people don't trust cops.''

''That's because they don't know you.'' She had

lifted her hand to his cheek. "I don't know how to thank you for all you've done."

If she'd known about his checkered past, she wouldn't trust him, either. Shaken by her confidence, he had cupped her hand in his and pressed his lips against the satin smoothness of her palm. "The sooner we get under way, the sooner we'll find Brittany."

Three miles west of the barrier island known as Sunset Bay Beach, he turned *Heavenly Days* parallel to shore and headed north toward the exclusive waterfront community where Swinburn had lived.

Glancing at Angel beside him on the flying bridge, the wind whipping her short brown hair across her face, he remembered her gratitude earlier on the dock, and responsibility dragged at him like an anchor. She was thankful now, but if he let her down, as he had Jenny a year ago, she wouldn't be grateful.

She'd be dead.

ANGEL GAZED ACROSS the water at the Mediterranean mansion sprawled over several acres of landscaped grounds. Barely visible beneath the towering crowns of banyans, the impressive house brought back no memories, only a curious and uncomfortable indifference, as if all her emotions had been sucked dry.

"You're certain this is the right place?"

Jordan nodded and steered the boat toward the dock at the foot of three graduated terraces that led to the house. "Michael said you lived here with

Swinburn from the time of your marriage three years ago until eighteen months later, when you filed for divorce.''

She wished she could feel *something*. Even her unbearable longing for Brittany would be an improvement over the strange numbness in her heart. She longed for the incredible excitement she'd experienced last night, first from Jordan's kiss, and later from the pleasure of his body molded against hers while they'd hidden in the utility closet. Even with their lives in danger, he had roused her senses, making her want him with a fierceness that had frightened her. The unmistakable hardness of his arousal against her had indicated he'd felt the same.

Now she felt nothing but emptiness. The sight of the imposing house had dampened all her responses.

''Michael does his research,'' she replied belatedly to Jordan's brief recital of her marriage history.

''Not research.'' His irrepressible grin gleamed beneath the bill of his ball cap, contrasting the white of his teeth with the depth of his tan. ''Michael moved in the same social circles as you and your ex-husband.''

''Did Michael also tell you the grounds for my divorce?''

Jordan frowned, but whether in uneasiness over discussing her divorce or in concentration as he approached the dock, she couldn't tell.

''Florida has a no-fault divorce law, but you charged Swinburn with mental cruelty.''

Instantly her numbness disappeared. Anxiety

buzzed in her head and wet her palms, and her heart battered her breastbone. She wiped her hands on her olive-drab chino shorts and surveyed the estate once again.

This time she paid closer attention. In addition to the two-story stuccoed house with its red barrel-tiled roof, cloistered walks and Spanish arches almost hidden by tumbling vines of scarlet bougainvillea, the complex included a four-car garage with an upstairs apartment in the same architecture, and behind it, a commercial-size greenhouse.

As they neared the dock, a free-form swimming pool set in the lush tropical landscaping of the upper terrace came into view. A flagstone path led from the pool area around the north side of the house.

Suddenly, she was running down that pathway, running for her life. Curling tendrils of jasmine from the arbor overhead clutched at her, and she batted them aside. David was dead. Shot. Six bullets from her *gun—*

"Angel?"

The memory evaporated in the hot morning sun, leaving her sick and shaken. She had killed David Swinburn with her own gun and run away. Michael and Jordan—especially Jordan—had been kind and helpful, but how would they treat her when they discovered she really had murdered her ex-husband?

"Angel, are you okay?"

She forced the taut muscles of her face to smile. "I'm fine."

Jordan was scrutinizing her with his policeman's

look that missed nothing. "Did you remember something?"

"Not a thing," she lied, "but maybe meeting the staff will jog my memory."

If it weren't for Brittany, she would have refused to disembark, fearful of what the people who had worked for David might reveal about her guilt. But she had to question the staff to find her daughter. She prayed silently that Brittany was safe, that she would find her quickly so she could let her daughter know her mother loved her.

How can I tell Brittany her mother killed her father?

She didn't have an answer.

Leaping onto the dock, she helped Jordan secure the boat at the pilings on the lower terrace. Together they climbed the quarried stone steps toward the house, then followed the flagstone walkway to the rear of the estate. On the pathway that she'd remembered, she braced herself for more flashes of memory, more jeers from her conscience. None came.

In a large cobbled courtyard between the house and garages, a tall, thin man with graying hair and angular features, including a hooked nose of amazing proportion, was washing a dark blue Lincoln Town Car. At their approach, he dropped his sponge into a bucket of soapy water and dried his hands on a towel.

"This is private property," he said in clipped British tones. "I'll have to ask you to leave."

Jordan stepped closer and showed his identification. "I'm an investigator for Attorney Michael Winslow's office. Detective Henderson has given us permission to talk to Mr. Swinburn's staff.''

The man's expression remained suspicious. ''I'm Henry Erskine, Mr. Swinburn's chauffeur.''

He looked past Jordan and his gray eyes met hers. He did a double take, and his face lifted in a beaming grin. ''Bless me! It's Miz Sara! We thought you were in jail.''

''I almost was, but—''

''Fiona, come down here,'' the man bellowed toward an open window in the apartment above the garage. ''It's Miz Sara! She's come back. Looks different, but it's her, all right.''

A door slammed, footsteps pattered on a staircase half-hidden on the side of the building, and a short, plump woman emerged around the corner and rushed toward her.

''Miz Sara.'' The white-haired woman with periwinkle-blue eyes and apple-red cheeks grabbed Angel's hands. ''I didna think we'd ever see you again.''

At the Scottish burr in Fiona's voice and the warmth of her greeting, Angel experienced an inexplicable surge of affection, but whether her fondness for the woman was a memory or a natural response to Fiona's friendly personality, she couldn't tell.

''I knew they wouldna keep you in jail,'' Fiona gushed. ''Anyone who knows you knows you didna kill Mr. Swinburn.''

Angel's self-loathing resurfaced. What would this

sweet, gentle woman think when she learned the truth?

Jordan, unaware of Angel's inner turmoil, introduced himself to Fiona. "I have some questions for you and your husband."

"We'll be happy to answer," Fiona said. "Won't we, Henry?"

"Anything to help Miz Sara," Henry agreed. "Come up. Fiona was just fixing tea."

"Or coffee, if you like," the housekeeper offered. "And I've baked sweet buns."

Minutes later, seated on the Erskines' porch, which overlooked the gulf, Angel balanced a cup of fragrant lemon tea on her lap and declined a rich bun. "I've lost my memories, Mrs. Erskine, and I need your help."

"Oh, my. You canna remember anything?"

Wishing she hadn't remembered killing David, Angel shook her head and blinked back tears. "I have to find Brittany. Do you have any idea where she is?"

Mr. and Mrs. Erskine exchanged a long, mournful look, and Angel's stomach tightened with apprehension. They knew something, and, judging by their expressions, it wasn't good.

"Whatever you can tell us," Jordan prodded, "would help."

Fiona looked to Henry again, and he nodded.

"Well," she said to Angel, "you called me Saturday afternoon, right before we left for our weekend visit with our son. You wanted to know if Brittany was here.''

''Was she?'' Angel asked.

Fiona shook her head. ''Mr. Swinburn had his daughter at the house Friday afternoon—I helped him keep an eye on her—but Saturday morning after breakfast, he put the wee lass and her baggage in the car—''

''Said he'd drive himself,'' Henry added. ''Had me secure the child carrier in the back seat of the Lincoln, and they drove out, just the two of them, about ten o'clock.''

Fiona looked close to tears. ''Miss Brittany wasna with him when he came back.''

Jordan set aside his tea and leaned forward. ''What time did Swinburn return?''

''About two o'clock.''

''That narrows our search down to a radius of *only* a hundred miles,'' Jordan said with a scowl.

Tortured by tearstained images of her daughter, Angel said, ''Do you know where he went? Did he give any hint where he might have taken her?''

Henry's angular features brightened. ''Now that you mention it, yes, he did leave a clue to where he'd been.''

''Where?'' Angel begged.

''I don't know where exactly, but I can point you in the right direction. South.''

''South?'' Jordan looked skeptical. ''How can you be certain he went south?''

''You saw me washing the car?''

Jordan nodded. "But what's that got to do with—"

"Medflies," Henry said with an emphatic nod.

"Medflies?" Angel and Jordan asked together.

Henry smiled. "You think I've gone 'round the bend, but I'm serious. Citrus groves near Fort Myers have had an outbreak of Mediterranean fruit flies—"

"Which they control by aerial spraying with malathion," Jordan said, comprehension dawning in his expression.

"That's right," Henry said, "and when I took the Lincoln out of the garage for its weekly wash this morning, I found spots in the paint caused by residue from the spray. Mr. Swinburn must have been on the road when the helicopters were spraying."

"So David took Brittany somewhere near Fort Myers?" Angel looked to Jordan for confirmation.

"Or he could have dropped her off somewhere else before driving to Fort Myers on some other errand."

Disappointed, Angel turned back to Fiona. "I don't understand. Why did he take Brittany away?"

Sadness filled Fiona's eyes. She shook her head and uttered a sorrowful *tsking* sound. "You really don't remember, do you, dear?"

Angel bit her bottom lip to keep from weeping.

"It was plain, evil spite," the housekeeper said.

"Spite?" Jordan said. "Over what?"

Fiona and Henry traded pained looks.

"Tell them," Henry said to his wife. "Our loyalty to Mr. Swinburn died when he did."

"He wanted to hurt you, Miz Sara. He was that furious when you divorced him, he wanted to make you pay for standing up to him."

Angel fought off an attack of dizziness. "You don't think he hurt her?"

"Oh, you mustn't fret yourself about that," Fiona said with a shake of her head.

"Right," Henry agreed. "Mr. Swinburn was a proper bastard, but he loved his little girl."

"If he loved her so much, then why exactly did he take the child away?" Jordan apparently shared her confusion.

Fiona's blue eyes turned bleary. "He wanted to punish Miz Sara for divorcing him. Defying him, he called it." She turned to Angel. "When you called me Saturday afternoon, you were crying so hard you could barely speak. You said Mr. Swinburn had called, telling you dinna bother to collect Miss Brittany at the end of the weekend, that he had hidden her away so you'd never see her again."

Jordan lunged forward and caught Angel's cup and saucer as it slid from her lap.

David Swinburn had not only stolen her daughter. He'd given her a perfect reason to want him dead.

Chapter Seven

Jordan observed Angel's horrified reaction to the Erskines' explanation of Brittany's disappearance and, despite his surge of sympathy, attempted to assess it objectively.

Swinburn's cruelty provided a strong motive for Angel to kill her ex-husband. If the Erskines had revealed that information to Maggie Henderson and her investigators, the state attorney's office would have a field day with it, and Michael Winslow's defense of Angel would be that much tougher.

Judging from her deathly pallor, she had drawn her own inference from the housekeeper's report and apparently believed she had murdered Swinburn.

Jordan couldn't blame her for jumping to that conclusion. Swinburn's attitude toward his ex-wife and daughter had given rise to Jordan's overpowering dislike of the man. Unfortunately, Swinburn's capacity for inflicting mental anguish on his wife hadn't ended with his life. The sooner Jordan could return Brittany safely to Angel, the sooner he could gather proof of her innocence and set her mind at ease.

The possibility existed, of course, that she *had* killed Swinburn in her desperation to recover her daughter, but the odds on that were slim to none. Despite the display of temper he'd witnessed, Angel didn't seem the type to lose control and commit murder in a frenzy of rage. If her natural disposition hadn't been cool and collected, she couldn't have handled the stresses of amnesia and her arrest and court appearance as well as she had.

Nor did she seem capable of killing in cold blood—unless he had lost completely his ability to assess character. She had never exhibited the slightest hint of malice or mean-spiritedness. Even now, she voiced no bitterness toward Swinburn.

Placing Angel's cup and saucer on the wicker tea table, he turned to the Erskines. "Did you tell the police Swinburn had taken the child away?"

Fiona's ruddy cheeks flushed darker. "They already knew. Miz Sara had reported her missing to Detective Panowski."

"Did Swinburn have friends or relatives in the area he could have left Brittany with?" Jordan asked.

Fiona shook her head. "We've worked for Mr. Swinburn ten years, ever since we came from England, and he never mentioned family other than his parents, who live on Turtle Key. They were the only kin who ever came to visit."

"We know the girl isn't there," Jordan explained. "According to detectives on the case, David's parents are the ones who told police the child was with

Angel. They insisted the report to Panowski was an attempt to defame their son.''

''Who is Angel?'' Fiona said.

''I call Sara Angel,'' Jordan explained. ''When I met her, she didn't know her name. I had to call her something.''

Fiona regarded him with a knowing look. ''I see.''

''Could David have taken Brittany to a friend's house?'' Angel asked.

The suffering etched on her face made Jordan wish she hadn't regained her memories of her daughter until after they'd found the little girl.

''Mr. Swinburn wasn't the kind of man to have intimate friends,'' Henry explained. ''He had some business associates with whom he socialized, but not friends in the best sense of the word. I know, because I served as both his butler and chauffeur.''

His answer seemed to squelch Angel's hope. Shoulders slumped and eyes glazed with misery, she stared out across the water, preoccupied with her thoughts.

Frustrated at his inability to relieve her unhappiness, Jordan returned his attention to the couple. ''Would Swinburn have taken Brittany to any of his business friends?''

Fiona shrugged her plump shoulders. ''He might have. He was a most unpredictable man.''

''Did he ever mention a man named James?'' Jordan asked.

The name roused Angel from her bleak musings. ''The men who tried to kidnap me and later searched my apartment are working for someone named James."

"First or last name?" Henry asked.

"I don't know," Jordan said. "It could be either."

Henry's face brightened. "Mr. Swinburn had a partner in his real estate firm, James Lassiter."

"I'd like to talk to this Lassiter," Jordan said. "Do you have his address?"

"I'll get it for you." Fiona disappeared into the apartment.

"If we're going to call on James Lassiter, I'll need a rental car," Jordan said. "May I borrow your phone book, Mr. Erskine?"

Henry looked puzzled. "Did you come in a taxi? I didn't hear it arrive."

Jordan shook his head. "My boat's moored at the dock. Is it okay to leave it there for now?"

"I don't see why not," Henry said. "And if you need transportation—"

"The Lincoln will attract too much attention," Angel said with a shake of her head.

Henry smiled, rearranging the angles of his long face. "I'm offering you my personal vehicle."

Clasping a sheet of pale blue writing paper, Fiona returned to the porch. "Here's Mr. Lassiter's home and business addresses and phone numbers." She handed the sheet to Jordan, then patted Angel's hand. "I do hope this Lassiter can help you find the wee lass."

Angel hoped so, too. Checking with David's partner was all they could do until Maggie Henderson allowed them access to the house and David's records.

FIFTEEN MINUTES LATER, Jordan sped through the main gates of the Swinburn estate on Henry's vintage Harley-Davidson. The chrome-and-black machine glinted in the sunlight, and behind him, Angel clutched his waist. Her distinctive features were hidden, like his, by the black-visored helmets, but they provided perfect disguises. Even Frank and Sidney wouldn't recognize them.

The surge of the powerful chopper reminded Jordan of his first assignment on the Sunset Bay department, working traffic control with the motorcycle squad. He had been green and idealistic, ready to make a serious dent in crime and disorderliness.

Jenny hadn't graduated from high school yet.

He opened the throttle, drowning his nostalgia in the distinctive roar of the Harley's engine. If he could find Brittany and clear Angel, he might atone in some small way for what had happened to Jenny.

And if he failed Angel as he had Jenny? He shoved the painful thought away, refusing to contemplate living with that outcome.

Before he and Angel left the Erskines, he had called the real estate office. Lassiter's secretary said he was out for the rest of the day, appraising a ranch for sale near Arcadia. Jordan expressed an interest in viewing the property as a prospective buyer, and she had given him the location.

As the sun rose toward noon, Jordan revved the

cycle beneath the overpass of I-75 on a two-lane country road and left the sprawling suburbs of Sunset Bay behind. Once they had exited the city, the air seemed fresher and cleaner. His somber mood, generated by unhappy memories, lifted, and for the first time since Jenny's death, he derived pleasure from his surroundings.

They passed several groves, some heavy with Valencia oranges and others emitting the heady perfume of orange blossoms. In one wide pasture, a herd of Brahman cattle gathered beneath the shade of a solitary tree. Nearer their destination, they crossed a bridge over the wide, crystal-clear waters of the Myakka River, its banks lined with live oaks and cabbage palms.

With Angel gripping his waist and the seductive heat of her breasts against his back, he imagined a languorous picnic on the riverbank before making love to her and watching passion darken the brown of her eyes beneath the shade of oaks shrouded in Spanish moss.

The vortex of a passing truck, hauling citrus to a concentrate plant, shook the cycle and blasted his daydream to shreds. Just as well. The detachment he'd struggled to maintain since he first met Angel had never been more essential. With two killers on her trail, one slight distraction, as on the night Jenny had died, could precipitate instant and irrevocable disaster.

Angel tugged on his sleeve and pointed ahead. A weathered wooden sign indicated the entrance to the property where they'd been told they'd find James Lassiter. Jordan slowed for the turn, then accelerated up a long, sandy driveway to a cracker-style house with a tin roof and broad, covered porches, set among a stand of pines.

His senses heightened. If James Lassiter was Frank and Sidney's boss, Jordan would soon find himself face-to-face with the man who wanted Angel dead. Angel's midriff, pressed against his waist, reminded him of the absence of his gun. Unable to rely on its protection, he concentrated on his surroundings, alert to any sign of danger.

In front of the house, Jordan parked the cycle behind a black BMW, the only vehicle in sight. He hopped off and removed his helmet. Angel dismounted and tugged off her helmet.

"Hello!"

From around the corner of the house, a tall and lanky stranger appeared, dressed in khaki slacks, a green golf shirt and tasseled loafers.

He approached them in the drive. "You folks shopping for property?"

"James Lassiter?" Jordan said.

"That's right. The office send you?" He stuck out his large hand and plastered a phony salesman's smile on his gaunt face.

"In a manner of speaking." Jordan shook his hand and scanned the property, making certain Lassiter was alone. "I'm Jordan Trouble, an investigator for Michael Winslow."

Lassiter's smile froze, then melted into a distrustful glare. "What do you want with me?"

"I'm looking for my daughter," Angel said. "I'm Sara Swinburn."

Lassiter's expression softened. "Sorry, didn't recognize you at first, Sara. Your hair's different. But why come to me looking for your child?"

"Before David died, he hid Brittany from me. You were his partner, so I thought—hoped—he had told you where he took her."

Lassiter glowered. "David may have been my partner, but he damned sure wasn't my friend. I only recently discovered he embezzled over a hundred thousand dollars from the office accounts. You did me a favor, Sara. If you hadn't killed him, he would have stolen me blind." Lassiter's face darkened with rage. "And if he hadn't been dead already, I might have killed him myself when my accountant uncovered the theft."

"My daughter—" Angel appeared close to tears.

"Do you know anything about Ms. Swinburn's daughter?" Jordan demanded.

Lassiter relented and abandoned his scowl, apparently touched by Angel's distress. "I'm sorry, Sara. I can't help with your little girl. I hadn't talked to David in weeks."

"Any objection to my searching David's office?" Jordan asked. "He might have left some record of Brittany's whereabouts."

"Be my guest. And if you don't find anything there, ask his secretary."

"She's working today?" Jordan said.

Lassiter's lips curled in disgust. "She better not be. I fired her over the embezzlement. Figured she was in on it with David. The two of them were very…close, if you know what I mean."

Jordan raised his eyebrows and wondered if David's secretary had been part of the reason for Angel's divorce. "Swinburn and his secretary were having an affair?"

"For the past five years." Lassiter slid a bewildered glance at Angel's stunned expression. "Sorry, Sara. It wasn't my place to intrude."

"Can I have the secretary's name and address?" Jordan asked.

"Bunny Shelton. I don't know where she lives, but she should be in the phone book."

"Listed under Bunny?" Jordan said doubtfully.

Lassiter shook his head. "Under her husband's name, Jim Shelton."

"*James* Shelton?" Angel's eyes met Jordan's, and he knew what she was thinking. Another James. If Lassiter hadn't hired killers to track her, maybe Shelton had.

"Yeah." Lassiter's look was puzzled. "You know him?"

"Never heard of the guy. Do you know any other friends or associates of Swinburn's who were named James?"

Lassiter's eyes narrowed. "Why?"

"Just a tip we had about who might have Brittany."

The Realtor thought for a moment, then shook his head. "Sorry."

Jordan swung onto the cycle, and Angel climbed behind him. "We won't take any more of your time. Thanks for your help."

"No problem. By the way, in your investigation, if you come across what David did with my money—"

"I'll let you know." Jordan started to put on his helmet, then stopped. "Just one more question."

"Yeah?"

"Do you know two guys named Frank and Sidney?"

Lassiter shrugged. "I know a couple of Franks, but no Sidney. Why?"

Jordan gauged Lassiter's response. He was either telling the truth or the world's best liar.

"It's not important. Thanks again."

Jordan made a sweeping survey of the outbuildings and the windows of the apparently deserted house before turning his back on them, then pulled on his helmet and gunned the cycle toward the highway.

AFTER THREE HOURS of digging through files in David's luxurious downtown office, every muscle in Angel's body ached. She rolled her shoulders and stretched, but the physical soreness was nothing compared to the pain in her heart. Every minute that passed without Brittany weighed on her chest like a rock slide, suffocating her with worry.

"You haven't eaten." Jordan closed the drawer of the file cabinet he'd been searching and pointed to a submarine sandwich, untouched on the desk in front of her.

She shook her head. "I'm not hungry."

She couldn't force food past the anxiety that constricted her throat. From the corner of David's desk, a brass-framed collage of Brittany's snapshots reproached her inadequacy and tortured her with memories—Brittany feeding seagulls at the beach, shaking hands with Mickey at Disney World, riding her first tricycle and pirouetting in her red velvet Christmas dress.

"Remember what Mrs. Erskine said?"

She started at Jordan's words. Staring at her daughter's pictures, she had forgotten he was in the room. "What?"

"Swinburn's housekeeper insisted he loved Brittany and wouldn't have done anything to harm her."

"Except steal her from her mother." Bitterness almost choked her. "We haven't uncovered a single clue to where she could be."

Jordan crossed the room and perched on the corner of the desk. "No clues on Brittany, but we did find another James."

"Carleton James?" Although she had come across the name in David's personal telephone directory, Jordan hadn't located anything in the office files to indicate the man had been David's client.

Jordan's midnight-blue eyes glowed with interest.

"The mysterious Carleton James, a multimillionaire whose source of income is a well-guarded secret."

"How do you know all that?"

"When I worked fraud, we had a former accountant on the team who could follow money trails like a bloodhound. Rooted out the income and outgo of every high roller in the county. *Except* Carleton James. Our mystery man, one of the county's greatest philanthropists, seen in the limelight only at every charitable function and never anywhere else, is lousy with dough that seems to materialize out of nowhere."

"But nothing connects him to Brittany?"

He leaned forward and smoothed the back of his hand down her cheek in a comforting but sensuous gesture that vibrated her nerve endings like the plucked strings of a guitar. "If he hired Frank and Sidney to kill you, he may also be responsible for Swinburn's murder."

The brief excitement of Jordan's touch withered and died, and she avoided facing him. Carleton James hadn't killed David. *She* had. But if she confessed to Jordan, in his disgust with her, he might abandon the search for Brittany, and she couldn't risk that. Once her daughter was in her arms again, Angel promised herself, she would come clean with Jordan and her attorney and face the consequences. But not before Brittany was safe.

"Why are you doing this?" She forced herself to meet his gaze.

"Searching the office?"

"Helping me."

"You came looking for me, remember?" He almost pulled off his attempt at nonchalance, but in spite of his casual tone and self-deprecating smile, the pain she remembered from their first meeting filled his eyes.

"You didn't have to help me. You could have said no."

"Nobody else was around to give you a hand, so you could say I was elected by default."

"You could have backed out anytime, or handed me over to Michael or any of your detective friends, but you didn't. Why stick with someone who is—" she faltered, almost blurting out her guilt "—who might be a killer?"

He dropped his cavalier manner. The agony in his eyes spread across his face, and his voice thrummed with unfamiliar intensity. "Let's just say there's another angel I owe a debt to. By helping you, who knows? Maybe I can clear my tab."

Shaken by his admission and anguished expression, she turned away, pulled a wastepaper basket from beneath the desk and swept her uneaten sandwich into it. "Let's find Bunny Shelton. Maybe David left Brittany with her."

"Whoa! Hold on." Jordan grabbed the trash basket and pulled out the sandwich.

She stared, puzzled. "If you were that hungry, all you had to do was ask."

He didn't stop with the submarine but continued

to remove wadded pieces of paper from the trash and smooth each one on the desk.

"My investigative skills are rustier than I thought," he admitted, continuing his search. "The trash should have been the first place I checked. Sometimes I find my best clues in the garbage."

His enthusiasm was contagious, and she joined him in retrieving and examining the discarded papers. "Why wasn't the trash emptied before now? The office looks as if it was cleaned recently."

"The basket was shoved into the kneehole and the cleaning crew probably missed it." He scanned the top of the page he had just opened. "Pay dirt!"

Her pulse quickened. "Something about Brittany?"

When he finished reading, his excitement deserted him, and a disquieting somberness took its place. Folding the paper quickly, he shoved it in the breast pocket of his sport shirt.

"What is it?" she demanded.

"Just a little something I'll check out later."

"You're making the same mistake you made before."

"What's that?" As if attempting to distract her from his find, he flashed a crooked grin, appealing enough under different circumstances to melt her heart.

But she was on to his trick. If he had been born a dog instead of a human, with his dark, soulful eyes and sun-kissed skin and hair, he would have been a playful golden Labrador, diverting attention from any misbehavior with his dynamic charm.

His smile widened under her scrutiny, confirming her appraisal. Definitely a golden Lab, with a wagging tail and winning way that would guarantee endless handouts and frequent liaisons with the canine equivalent of femmes fatales in backyards all over town.

Resisting the impulse to return the grin, she refused to allow his devil-may-care charisma to deter her—not when her daughter's life was at stake.

"Something significant is on that paper," she said, holding out her hand, "and I need to know what it is."

"I don't want you to worry about it." His smile didn't waver. "Let me check it out first."

"You can't keep it from me."

Lunging for the paper in his pocket, she tripped over the leg of the desk and stumbled against him. He locked his arms around her, breaking her fall against the broad expanse of his chest.

With her face crushed to his neck, the thundering tempo of his pulse vibrated through her, magnified by the sizzling heat of his skin. A virile combination of sunshine, sea and masculinity filled her nostrils, and hot longing zigzagged through her like high voltage. Shaken by her involuntary response, she pushed away and regained her feet.

His look of boyish, lovable charm had disappeared. No longer the affable golden Lab, he'd become a sensuous, powerful and dangerous wolfhound. Desire flushed his face and burned in his eyes like blue flames, igniting a corresponding conflagration deep inside her.

Her hand still rested against his chest where she had braced herself to push away, and the paper in his pocket crinkled, reminding her of Brittany. She snatched her hand back as if the contact had burned.

What was wrong with her? What kind of mother surrendered to seduction when her daughter needed her?

The same kind of mother who killed her daughter's father.

Her passion dispersed beneath the cold dousing of logic. With a swift flick of her hand, she removed the paper from his pocket and moved away to read it.

''Angel, don't!''

The tension in his voice flooded her with fear and made her pause. ''Why shouldn't I read this? What's so terrible about it?''

He pulled her back into his arms, this time with a tenderness at odds with his previous urgency. ''It may not mean anything, but I don't want you to worry. Please, let me look into it.''

She was tired of operating in the dark, without memories to guide her. She wanted facts, no matter how distressing they might be. Twisting in his embrace until her back was against his chest, she unfolded the sheet of watermarked stationery to find Carleton James's letterhead engraved at the top.

"'Swinburn, return what's mine,'" she read aloud, "'or I will take what's yours.'"

"Cryptic, isn't it?" Jordan's arms tightened around her waist.

She forced herself to voice her fear. "Do you think he was talking about Brittany?"

"I'll have to watch his house for signs of her. Talk to his employees. Eventually question James himself."

"I'm going with you."

She sensed the refusal in his stillness before he spoke. "That's not a good idea."

"Why not?"

"For one thing, interrogating James won't be easy."

"What do you mean?"

"I can't just waltz up to the front door and ask if he kidnapped Brittany Swinburn. If he did..."

"Go on."

"Then he's a dangerous man who should be avoided at all costs. Besides, he won't admit to taking Brittany. I'll have to search for her."

"She's my child, and I'm going with you. I don't care *how* dangerous James is."

He pivoted her by the shoulders to face him. "The potential for disaster is too great. I'll take you back to the boat while I snoop around James's place."

Carleton James didn't frighten her. The devil himself wasn't any scarier than the prospect of someone hurting Brittany. Not even the trial and her almost certain conviction for David's murder frightened Angel more. She had to find her daughter, assure her safety and locate someone who would love her and care for her when her mother went to jail.

She tipped her chin and locked gazes with Jordan. "If you don't take me with you, I'll go alone."

AFTER LEAVING the real estate office, they sought out the address listed for James Shelton in the local telephone directory and found his dilapidated house at the end of a dead-end road in a deteriorating neighborhood. Knee-high weeds and grass choked the yard, cracks riddled the front walk, and the torn screens of the front porch hung in gray curls.

Bunny Shelton answered their knock, but didn't open the screen door. "What do you want?"

Jordan assessed the woman with hair the texture of straw, red-rimmed eyes, wrinkled shorts and shirt and teeth and fingers stained with nicotine and wondered what had driven Swinburn to cheat on Angel.

Jordan introduced himself, then Angel, using her real identity.

Definitely not the soft and cuddly creature of her name, Bunny was all sharp angles and barbed tongue. "You got some nerve coming here, Sara Swinburn, after killing the only man I ever loved."

Angel's eyes flashed with anger. "I wasn't aware Mr. Shelton was dead."

"Jim's alive and kicking—unfortunately. The good news is the commercial fishing boat he works on has been out for three weeks and won't be back for three more. I'm talking about Dave, your *ex*-husband.''

If Jim Shelton had really been at sea for three weeks, that crossed him off their list of suspects, Jordan thought. Besides, from the looks of the Shelton house, the owner couldn't afford hired killers like Frank and Sidney.

''I'm not here to trade insults.'' Angel was making an obvious effort to hide her dislike and be conciliatory. ''I'm looking for my daughter. Do you have her?''

Bunny's hatchet-shaped features contorted in a scowl. ''Dave never let me near his precious daughter. Figured I wasn't good enough for her.''

''Did he say where he'd taken her?'' Angel asked.

''Last time I saw Dave was Friday morning. He was on his way to your place to pick up the kid.''

Bunny glared at Angel with hate-filled eyes, and Jordan tensed, ready to spring to Angel's defense if the woman shoved open the door and attacked.

''And even if I *did* know,'' Bunny continued in a high-pitched voice as annoying as electronic feedback on a sound system, ''you're the last person I'd tell.''

''Maybe you'll tell the police,'' Jordan suggested with the hint of a threat.

''Yeah, if I knew. But I don't. Now get off my property before I call the cops myself.''

''Just one more question. Do you know a man named Carleton James?''

Fear drained the angry color from Bunny's thin face. She shook her head.

"Then why does his name frighten you?" Jordan asked.

Bunny licked her thin lips nervously. "Dave told me if I ever so much as mentioned that name, he'd kill me."

"David actually threatened to *kill* you?" Angel lifted her feathery eyebrows in surprise.

Clutching her sleeveless blouse at her throat, Bunny nodded. "Yeah, but I didn't believe him. Dave wasn't the violent type, you know? But he said if he didn't kill me, the man you just named would."

Weighing the secretary's words and body language, Jordan concluded she must be telling the truth. "Is Carleton James the violent type?"

"I dunno. But he gives me the heebie-jeebies. If a snake could talk, it'd sound just like him."

"Did James come to the office often?" Jordan said.

"Never. He used to call once a month, until lately."

"And latcly?"

"He telephoned two, sometimes three times a day for the last few weeks."

"That's all you know about James?"

"That's it. Never laid eyes on him."

As if suddenly realizing she'd said too much, Bunny balled her hands on her hips and glared at them through the torn screen of the door. "Are you leaving now, or do I have to call the cops?"

JORDAN AND ANGEL RETURNED to the boat to wait until nightfall. He attempted once again to discourage her from accompanying him to visit Carleton James—but without success. When the sun set, they changed into dark clothing before heading for the exclusive country-club enclave on the other side of town from David Swinburn's waterfront home.

A pale, crescent moon hung in the starless sky and a westerly breeze carried the salty essence of the sea as Jordan eased back on the Harley's throttle and leaned into the turn onto the boulevard where James lived. Angel's arms tightened around his waist as she shifted balance with him. The pressure of her embrace and the delectable warmth of her body against his back brought both a surge of pleasure and renewed apprehension for her safety.

Scanning the exclusive neighborhood, he memorized the terrain and noted possible avenues of escape. Dense oaks lined the street and absorbed most of the light, providing plenty of places to hide.

A few houses from James's address, Jordan parked in the circular drive of a residence with heavily shuttered windows, whose owners had apparently returned north for the season, and gave Angel a hand to dismount.

"We'll walk from here," he said.

Her earlier threat to come alone if he didn't bring her with him had left him with only two choices, both potentially deadly, and he'd chosen the latter as the lesser danger. With her, he could at least keep an eye on her. Since the night they met, he had rebelled against taking responsibility for her, especially when her reliance on him for protection had reactivated the nightmares that led to his excessive drinking a year ago.

Now an unrelenting thirst for the numbing balm of alcohol consumed him, brought on by his growing fear for Angel's safety. He'd lost what little objectivity toward her he'd had in the beginning, and that loss hurt his chances of protecting her.

She was no longer simply a stranger in need of assistance. He was falling in love with her. Her extraordinary good looks had captured him from the start, but he'd soon learned her beauty was more than skin-deep. Her remarkable courage, her fierce love for her child, her composure under the disturbing circumstances of her amnesia and her unique, gentle charm had cast a spell he couldn't shake. Nor could he throw off his fear that, if a crunch came, he'd let her down.

He defied his body's demand for a drink to ease his anxiety. He had to remain sober for total vigilance and concentration, and he'd need every skill he'd learned as an officer to assure that no harm came to her. Doubt born of experience twisted in his gut. With Jenny, every resource he'd possessed hadn't been enough.

With a superhuman effort, he tamped down his self-doubts and dashed across the street with Angel into the shadows of the eight-foot brick wall that surrounded James's estate. Avoiding the streetlights by skirting the wall, they worked their way toward the main entrance with its locked wrought-iron gates.

He gazed through the opening across the circular drive that swept the front of the antebellum-style house. A light shone behind drawn draperies of a downstairs room and another gleamed upstairs at the front corner of the house, but he couldn't tell if anyone was inside.

"Should you ring the bell?" Angel pointed to a recessed panel in the wall beside the gate.

"I want to look around before James knows we're here. If he has Brittany, I don't want to give him time to hide her."

Angel tilted her head and surveyed the barricade. "If we climb the gate, someone will see us, and if we go over the wall, the pyracantha thorns will slash us to ribbons. What do we do now?"

"Check for a rear entrance."

In the darkness of the towering wall, they crept around a corner and down the next block until they came to a break in the brick expanse, spanned by another wrought-iron gate.

A hundred feet inside the compound, a multicar garage attached to the rear of the main house was barely visible in the faint moonlight.

"Can we risk climbing this gate?" Angel asked softly.

He shook his head and pointed to a speaker box and the touch pad of a security system. "Not without setting off an alarm."

"But Brittany might be in there." She considered

the bristling, thorn-laden vines covering the walls on both sides of the gate. It would take more than stickers to keep her from her daughter. "We'll have to go over the wall."

Abruptly, a loud electronic hum, followed by a metallic rattle, broke the stillness. Jordan yanked Angel facedown beneath a cluster of lady palms beside the gate. In the compound, a slit of light appeared at the foundation of the garage and widened into a bright rectangle as an automatic door lifted. A well-tuned engine purred to life, headlights flashed, and a car pulled out of the garage and headed down the broad drive toward the gate.

Flattened against the ground with his arm around Angel, Jordan watched the car's approach. The electronic lock of the gate clicked, the wrought-iron barricades swung inward, and a sedate black limo passed through, onto the street. The limo's tinted windows hid the occupants.

When the car had rounded the corner, Jordan leapt to his feet and tugged Angel with him. "Follow me. Hurry!"

The gates had almost closed. Jordan pushed Angel through the narrowing opening, then plunged through himself. A few seconds later and the gates would have crushed him. He veered off the driveway and joined Angel among the low, spreading branches of a Norfolk Island pine.

"Look!" She grabbed his sleeve and pointed toward the lowering garage door that was quickly obscuring their view of the well-lighted garage.

"Is someone in there?" All he'd seen before the automatic door dropped completely was an empty space next to a compact red sedan.

"I saw...I remember..." Her hand trembled on his arm.

"What is it?"

"That car..." Her voice quaked as violently as the rest of her.

"The limo?"

"No, the one in the garage, the red Nissan."

The description sounded familiar, but before he could identify it, she spoke again.

"That's *my* car."

Chapter Eight

"*Your* car?" Jordan said. "Are you sure?"

"I remember driving it," Angel whispered, "and the plate on the front bumper has my initials, SWS. No wonder the police couldn't find it if it's been locked in James's garage all this time."

"How'd it get there, and why?"

Her breath hissed between her teeth, and her grip on his arm tightened. "You don't suppose I...?"

"You what?"

"What if I *know* Carleton James? What if I went to him after—" She broke off abruptly, as if afraid to voice the words.

"After David died?"

She nodded and spoke in a soft, pained voice. "Maybe *I* left my car here."

Angel in cahoots with Carleton James? The troublesome thought gnawed at Jordan.

So far, his investigation had raised more questions than answers. He struggled against his growing affection for Angel to keep his mind open to all possibilities, including her guilt, and peered into the inky blackness, alert for watchdogs or security guards.

Until now, James had been merely a potential suspect, but Angel's car in his garage turned tonight's sortie into a whole new ball game. James had something to hide, and people with dangerous secrets often went to extreme lengths, such as hiring killers to make certain those secrets stayed hidden.

Angel fidgeted beside him, "Aren't we going to check the house to see if Brittany's there?"

He scooted deeper into the branches and tugged her with him. "For now, we wait."

"Wait?" Impatience rang in her whisper. "For what? The limo to come back? Let's go in while it's gone."

"We won't wait long. Trust me." Jordan almost choked on his words. How could he expect her to trust him when he didn't trust himself?

He checked his watch, then continued his observation of the dark grounds. He had estimated the estate's perimeter and how long the slowest circuit by a patrolling guard, either human or canine, might take. When that much time had passed, he and Angel would approach the house, but not before. With luck, the limo wouldn't return in the meantime.

He folded his arms around Angel, drew her against him and waited. Her silky hair tickled his nose, and the subtle fragrance matched the scent of honeysuckle on the night breeze. Her soft curves molded against him, and longing spiked in his groin.

Focus, Trouble. Stay alert.

He clamped his teeth on the soft tissue of his cheek and welcomed the pain that squelched his desire and cleared his head. Yielding to the temptation in his arms could get them both killed. The minutes dragged by until a final check of his watch told him it was time to move.

They slipped from beneath the branches and raced up the dark driveway toward the garage. Jordan checked the doors. All locked. At the sudden crash of shattering glass, he froze, and Angel halted beside him.

"Dammit, Sidney, you broke it." The angry shout carried across the lawn from the house. "Give me that beer. I'll drink it from the can."

Pressing a finger to his lips to signal silence, Jordan moved toward the house's rear entrance. Angel followed at his heels to a back porch, apparently off the kitchen, where windows were raised to the mild night air.

Hiding with Angel behind a large camellia bush just ten feet from an open window, Jordan could see Frank, sitting at the kitchen table, while Sidney rummaged through a commercial-size refrigerator and emerged with his arms full.

"I don't care if I break every glass in his house," Sidney said. "*Mr.* James goes prancing off to a charity event, as usual, dressed to the nines, and tells *us* to get back to work."

"He's the boss," Frank reminded him.

"Well, boss or not, a man's got to eat."

"Then eat, for Pete's sake, and let's get out of here. We have our orders."

Sidney deposited his armload onto the table and picked up a table knife. "So what's new? We've had those stinkin' orders for days."

"If we find her daughter, Sara Swinburn will have to. come to us." Frank took a drink from a can of beer. "And once she does, James will threaten to kill the kid if Mrs. Swinburn doesn't tell him what he needs to know."

"Yeah, yeah," Sidney grumbled, slathering bread with brown mustard and piling on cold cuts. "I know the drill."

"Naturally, James will kill them *both* after he's forced the truth from her."

"It ain't James who offs 'em."

Frank exhaled a dramatic sigh. "That's what he pays us for. Killing is a skill. Not like cutting grass or cleaning a pool. Any moron can do that."

"I ain't never killed a kid, and I don't like thinking about it. It's enough to spoil my appetite."

Swallowing his revulsion, Jordan cast a quick glance at Angel but couldn't read her expression in the darkness. He returned his attention to the argument in the kitchen.

Frank reached across the table and filched a cold cut from the platter. "James will spoil more than your appetite if we don't find that kid."

"Where we gonna look?" Sidney mumbled around a mouthful of sandwich. "We came up empty at her apartment, Swinburn's computer files told us zip and Trouble's boat has disappeared. How do we know he ain't got her and the kid with him?''

''We'll check with our man at the police department. He's always come through for us before.''

Jordan bit back a curse. Someone in the department was slipping James information, the leak Jordan had suspected when Spacek showed up so conveniently at Angel's hearing.

Frank finished his beer, wiped his mouth with a napkin and shoved away from the table. ''Get rid of this mess or Mrs. Gibbons will complain when she comes in tomorrow. I'd rather face James's wrath than hers.''

Frank left the kitchen through a swinging door, and Sidney flipped a finger at his partner's retreating back before stuffing the rest of the sandwich in his mouth. Jordan waited while he cleaned up the kitchen before leaving the room, licking mustard from his stubby fingers.

As soon as the kitchen lights clicked off, Jordan and Angel sprinted toward the rear gate.

''Into the trees,'' he told her softly.

Minutes later, another garage door rose, and a dark green Buick, with Frank at the wheel and Sidney in the passenger seat, rolled down the drive. The gates parted, and once the car had exited, Jordan and Angel skimmed through the opening onto the street before the iron barricades clanged shut behind them.

''Thank God, James doesn't have Brittany,'' Angel said as they hurried toward the house where they'd left the Harley, ''but I don't know where else to look.''

He grasped her hand and gave it a reassuring squeeze. ''We haven't searched your ex-husband's place yet. He could have left clues to where he took Brittany.''

She halted so quickly she almost threw him off balance. ''The police are combing the house. If they find something, James's spy will tell him where she is.''

Jordan stared into the brown depths of her eyes, glowing almost golden beneath the streetlights. ''You remembered your car tonight. Do you remember anything else?''

The guilt flitting across her face told him she was holding back, but she shook her head.

''If you can recall something, anything that will help us find Brittany—''

''Don't you think I'd tell you?''

The unfamiliar sharpness in her voice surprised him. ''We're both tired. After a good night's sleep we can think more clearly. Your memories are returning, a few at a time. Maybe tomorrow you'll remember more.''

As JORDAN STEERED *Heavenly Days* a few miles offshore from David's estate to drift for the rest of the night, Angel welcomed the noise of the boat's powerful engines, which drowned all expectations of discussion.

Later, alone in the wide double bed of the cabin

and hounded by a guilty conscience, she tossed restlessly. She regretted lying to Jordan about her memories, but she couldn't confess she'd killed David, not until Jordan had helped her find Brittany.

He had promised he would, and she didn't doubt him. He might fool others with his carefree attitude and charming grin, but she'd detected his inner strength, his determination and patience, and, above all, his concern for others, peeking through his casual facade. With those qualities, he must have been an outstanding cop, and she wondered if he would ever reveal why he'd left the force or share the events that caused the sorrow lurking in his eyes.

She groaned and buried her head beneath the pillow, but she couldn't hide from the fact she was falling in love with Jordan Trouble.

You're not telling him about killing David, her conscience taunted her, *because you know a cop could never love a murderer.*

To still the accusing voice, she rose, pulled a robe over her short gown and tiptoed past a sleeping Jordan, sprawled with his long, tanned legs tangled in the sheets of the bed folded out from the galley benches.

The glass doors of the lounge rolled open soundlessly, and she stepped onto the deck. The boat drifted peacefully on the calm gulf waters beneath a blue-velvet sky, where stars poked holes in the darkness now that the moon had set. To the east, the lights of Sunset Bay cast a glowing yellow dome over the city.

Her little girl was out there somewhere. She hoped Brittany was sleeping and not lying awake, crying for her mother. She yearned to hold her daughter, to breathe her sweet baby scent, watch dimples crease her cheeks when she smiled, feel the chubby arms around her neck and the tiny lips against her face.

I'll find you, sweetheart. I promise.

How she intended to keep that pledge, she had no idea. Sitting on the deck, still warm from the Florida sun, she clasped her knees to her chest and tried to ward off the pain, but she couldn't halt the relentless ache in her heart or the tears that coursed down her cheeks.

If separating her from her child was God's punishment for taking David Swinburn's life, she deserved the pain, but Brittany hadn't done anything wrong. Her innocent baby shouldn't have to suffer for her mother's sins.

The gentle swell of the waves rocked her but brought no comfort. If her surroundings were any indicator, she could be the only person in the universe. Water stretched in every direction as far as she could see, and above arched an infinite curve of dark sky, spangled with stars. Without her daughter, without family or memories or friends, she yielded to the overpowering solitude. If she disappeared that instant from the face of the earth, who would notice? Or care?

She didn't hear Jordan's approach, but suddenly he was there, lifting her by the elbows, scanning her face in the starlight.

"Couldn't sleep?" he asked.

Embarrassed at being caught wallowing in self-pity, she slipped from his grasp and made a furtive swipe at her cheeks with the backs of her hands. Shifting out of his arms' reach, she perched on the cushioned ice chest that lined the stern. "It's a beautiful night. I can't remember seeing so many stars before."

"Brittany is safe, and we'll find her. You have to believe that."

He had read her mind—or was she that transparent? Wearing only boating shorts, he stood like a bulwark between her and hopelessness. She longed to believe his assurances, but guilt prevented her.

The sins of the mother, the darkness whispered.

She shivered uncontrollably. If harm came to her daughter, she had only herself to blame. Tears she'd attempted to hide flowed faster, and she tried without success to stifle the sobs that shook her.

In the blink of an eye, Jordan settled beside her, pulled her onto his lap and into his arms. "Go ahead and cry if it makes you feel better."

"I despise weepy women," she said between sobs, "women who bawl their heads off, as if they're helpless to deal with their problems."

With a rare tenderness, he brushed her hair out of her face, then clasped her against the warmth of his bare chest and rocked her gently with the motion of the boat. "Handling problems is always tough, but especially without memories. Cut yourself some slack."

She shook her head but said nothing. He didn't understand her fear, and she didn't dare enlighten him.

"Besides," he added in a light tone, "according to the experts, crying's good for you."

"Right," she said wryly, between sniffles.

"It's true. Tears flush out chemicals caused by stress."

She was frustrated that she couldn't cease weeping or hiccuping. "Why is everything that's good for me so unpleasant?"

Still cradling her against his pliant warmth, he continued to rock her tenderly. "My grandmother—"

"The one whose cookies you stole?"

He nodded. "She insisted suffering makes you a better person."

"If I get any better," she said with irony and a sniffle, "I won't be able to stand myself."

His rich laugh echoed across the water. "Thatta girl. I knew you hadn't lost your spunk."

Warmed by his laughter, she felt her sobbing ease. Pulling away, she lifted her head and considered the man who held her. His eyes burned dark as the night sky, and his impressive profile created an enticing silhouette against the starscape.

"Why are you so good to me?" she asked, knowing she was undeserving.

"You bring out the best in me."

Her heart plummeted, and her tears threatened to return. "But you don't know me—"

"I know you well enough. And I like what I know."

"Don't jump to conclusions. Once you learn more—"

"I want to learn everything about you." His low voice carried a seductive urgency.

"What if you discover things you don't like?"

"Nobody's perfect, least of all me. I'll take the bad along with the good."

He lowered his head until his lips hovered inches from hers, and his warm breath fanned her cheek. Beneath her hands, splayed against his broad chest, his heart pounded with an insistent, primeval rhythm that stoked her blood, burning away reason and resistance. No longer alone, she reveled in the contact of flesh against flesh and the consuming heat that seared away her solitude.

"We shouldn't," she protested, not really meaning it.

"Shouldn't what?" His mouth curved in the devilish grin she'd grown to love.

She fought the desire that filled her. Deeper involvement wouldn't be fair to either of them. "We should go to bed."

His smile widened. "Sounds like a good idea."

"I meant go to sleep."

"Are you sleepy?"

Sleepy? When every cell in her body tingled with awareness? When every atom of her being called to him, begged him to oust her loneliness.

"Yes," she lied.

"I've wanted to make love to you from the first moment I saw you—" he brushed her lips with a butterfly kiss "—but I'll stop if you say so."

He raised his head, watching, waiting for her answer.

One small word would restrain him. Although she sensed the passion surging through him, she trusted his control. If she asked, he would honor her request.

But how could she say no when she wanted him as much as she'd ever wanted anything? She longed to lose herself in the excitement of his embrace, to express through actions the feelings she didn't dare voice, to *belong,* if only for a few fleeting minutes.

Most of all—and she condemned her selfishness—she wanted something wonderful to remember during the long, lonely prison nights that stretched inevitably ahead.

"Angel?"

The resonance of her name on his lips caressed her, toppling the last of her resistance.

"We can sleep," she whispered and lifted her face to him, "later."

With a low moan, he gathered her closer and claimed her mouth with his. Returning his kiss, she parted her lips, welcoming the taste of him, mingling their breath. He untied the belt of her robe with one hand and slid the other around to cup her breast. She surrendered willingly to his touch, glorying in the current that sizzled between them, uniting them, expunging her isolation, ending her exile.

Lifting her to her feet, he tossed the cushions from

the bench onto the deck, then lowered her onto them. With an apparent need for intimacy that matched her own, he tugged off her robe and gown and shrugged out of his shorts.

The cool gulf breeze rolled over them, steaming against the heat of their nakedness as he traced kisses from the hollow of her neck, across her breasts. When his mouth grazed the curve of her stomach, she curled her fingers in his hair and arched toward him.

His skin burned hot against hers, like a fiery blast of noonday Florida sun. She trailed her fingers across the granite hardness of his chest, over his washboard stomach and his ribs, down the firmness of his buttocks, relishing the feel of him. His latent strength and ruggedness formed the counterpart to her vulnerability and softness, two parts of a perfect whole.

She reveled in the comfort and security of his embrace, and her loneliness and solitude evaporated beneath the heat of his lips. But as his nibbling kisses teased her nipples, brushed her stomach and skimmed the insides of her thighs, comfort ignited and transformed into a deeper, more insistent force, forged into fiery desire by his touch.

Retracing the path of his lips with his fingers, he reached between her legs, stroking, fondling, until she shuddered with delight. The skillful movements of his fingers sent molten pleasure rippling through her veins, and she trembled wildly, mindlessly, racked by wave after wave of devastating sensation that left her gasping.

When she could breathe again, he knelt above her, dark blue eyes aflame.

"Angel." He breathed her name like a prayer.

Gladly, she opened herself to him, and he lowered his hips and slipped inside her with a slow, powerful drive that made her cry out with enjoyment. Clasping him closer, she was oblivious to everything but the pulsing thrust that joined them in a bond as old as time.

She refused to close her eyes, memorizing his face and recording the input of every sense—the cool breeze against her skin, the reassuring weight of his body on hers, the hot, masculine scent of him, mixed with the biting nip of salt water and seaweed, the rasp of canvas cushions at her back, the salty taste of him on her lips and the powerful, riveting plunge that shattered solitude and isolation. She savored it all, enough feelings and images to last a lifetime.

Despite wanting their lovemaking to last forever, she couldn't resist the tidal pull of passion that drew them closer, urged them forward on a cresting wave and flung them into the encircling dome of stars. Fiercely, tenderly, he cried her name, and it reverberated, like the heartbeat of the earth in the midnight darkness. Then the world flared like a supernova, and she exploded again in exquisite release.

Later, braced on the deck, he held her on his lap again and draped her robe around her against the cool night air. He traced the contours of her cheeks, then grasped her chin and tilted her face until their eyes met.

"No regrets?"

Tears of happiness and remorse filled her eyes. She couldn't answer. Whether she responded yes or no, either would be a lie.

"Angel?"

"Mmm," she murmured noncommittally, wrapped her arms around his neck and buried her face in the hollow of his throat.

Without another word, he rose with her in his arms and carried her to bed.

WHEN HE AWAKENED before dawn, Jordan cursed himself for the worst kind of fool and slid away from Angel, who was lying with her slender arm across his chest. He yanked on a pair of shorts and deck shoes and climbed to the flying bridge.

Relying on the stiff breeze to clear his head of the tantalizing image of Angel in his bed, he revved the powerful engine to maximum speed and headed toward shore.

He never should have allowed his involvement to progress this far. Any kind of relationship with Angel had been doomed from the start. She'd already been through hell, losing her daughter, accused of murder and suffering from memory loss. She didn't need him and his problems adding to her difficulties.

Not that he believed she'd killed her husband. With Frank and Sidney after her, the whole scheme had stunk of a setup from the beginning. Her car in Carleton James's garage was even stronger evidence that she'd been framed.

It wasn't her guilt that worried him.

It was his.

What could he, a burned-out former cop who had committed one of the most monumental screwups in the history of the department, who had seen his confidence shredded into nonexistence, offer a woman like her?

He couldn't support a wife and child on his security pay, couldn't even offer them a decent roof over their heads. And worst of all, he couldn't guarantee he'd stay sober, not with a stampede of screeching demons still on his heels.

He brooded all the way back to Swinburn's estate and hoped the stiff breeze would blow away his frustration. Docking the boat and connecting the hookups for water and electricity Henry had shown him the day before, he realized his disposition had returned to its usual gloomy level—until he heard Angel moving about below and his frustration reappeared with a vengeance.

When he entered the galley to fix breakfast, she was in the shower, and he fought his irrational longing to join her and resume where they'd left off last night. It had been a mistake then—it would be a disaster now.

That should never have happened. You knew from the get-go to keep your distance.

He had an excuse, just like every two-bit punk he'd ever arrested. But *his* excuse was a doozy. He'd been pitted against a force bigger than both of them. He sure as hell hadn't figured on falling in love.

"Hello!"

Flinching at the sudden but familiar shout, he scattered ground coffee across the countertop. With a quick swipe, he cleared the counter, inserted the basket into the coffeemaker and pressed the on switch before hurrying on deck.

Michael Winslow stood on the lower terrace, the jacket of his gray suit hooked by a thumb over his shoulder. Jordan welcomed his friend with a grin.

"Come aboard. Coffee'll be ready in a minute."

Michael leapt onto the deck with the grace of an athlete and followed Jordan into the lounge.

"Had breakfast?" Jordan asked.

"Been up since dawn, on the phone with Maggie."

Wearing Jordan's terry-cloth robe pulled tight at the waist, with the sleeves rolled back above her slender wrists, Angel stepped out of his cabin smelling of soap, honeysuckle and temptation. Jordan avoided her gaze, knowing Michael would read what his face couldn't hide.

"Morning," Michael greeted her.

Lucky for him, his gaze didn't linger. Friend or not, Jordan would have been tempted to punch out his lights if he'd looked at Angel the way Jordan was looking at her.

"You'd better hear this, too, Sara," Michael said when she headed toward the lower cabin.

Angel turned and shot Jordan a puzzled look. He shrugged to indicate he didn't know why Michael was there, pointed to the galley bench and, after she slid onto it, scooted beside her.

"Has your secretary located Brittany?" she asked, hope lighting her face like a beacon.

"Claire's called every name on the list, but no one could help us," Michael said gently.

The light in her eyes disappeared. Despite his earlier resolve to keep his distance, Jordan reached for her hand.

Michael sat across the table from them. "I came to fill you in on the evidence Maggie has in the Swinburn case."

Angel stiffened beside Jordan.

"Don't jump to conclusions, remember?" he warned her.

"It doesn't look good for the home team," Michael admitted solemnly.

Not wanting to frighten Angel, Jordan suppressed a shiver at his friend's tone. She already seemed nervous enough for both of them.

"Does Maggie have a case?" he asked Michael.

"Rock solid. Swinburn was shot with a gun he bought for Sara."

Jordan tightened his grip on Angel's hand. "So the evidence is circumstantial?"

"I wish," Michael said with a grimace. "Six shots at point-blank range. And only Sara's prints are on the gun."

"Witnesses?"

"A neighbor saw Sara fleeing the scene within the

time frame the medical examiner gives for Swinburn's death.''

"I did it," she confessed in a soft, flat voice. "I shot him."

Michael's eyebrows peaked in surprise. "You remember?"

"I...I think so."

"Do you remember why?" he asked quietly.

She shook her head. "All I get are...flashes. Bits and pieces."

Her face pale and trembling beneath the navy blue towel she'd wrapped turban-style over her wet hair, she wouldn't look at Jordan. He wondered if she had just remembered or if she'd known all along and hadn't told him. He rejected the latter possibility. Angel was no killer and no liar, either. If she *had* shot her husband, she must have had a damned good reason, like self-defense.

He rose and poured coffee for the three of them before resuming his seat. "When do I get access to the house?"

"Crime scene unit finished late last night," Michael said. "Which reminds me. They found something interesting."

Jordan groaned. "Give me some good news."

Michael sipped his coffee. "Don't know if it's good or bad, but the drive on Swinburn's computer was wiped clean."

"Goes to motive, doesn't it?" For the first time since Michael's disclosure of the evidence, Jordan felt a glimmer of hope. "Why would Angel kill her husband and erase all his records? It doesn't make sense.''

Michael checked his gold-and-stainless-steel Rolex, downed the rest of his coffee and stood. ''Making sense of all this is your job, Trouble. I have an appointment.''

Jordan walked with Michael to the edge of the terrace. When he returned, Angel had disappeared into his cabin and closed the door.

Slamming his mind against the seductive images of last night, he poured another cup of coffee. Crunch time had arrived. Not only did he have to protect Angel from James's hired killers, he had to prove her innocence against overwhelming evidence.

For someone who hadn't wanted the responsibility in the first place, he was drowning in it.

AN HOUR LATER, Angel reluctantly accompanied Jordan as he climbed the terraces toward Swinburn's mansion.

''I spoke with Fiona while you were dressing,'' he said. ''She promised to leave the doors unlocked for us.''

The skirt of her lemon-yellow sundress billowed in the sea breeze as Angel hesitated on the lower terrace. Last night in Jordan's arms had been almost perfect, but Michael's news had spoiled everything. Jordan knew now that *she* had shot David. When he entered the house, he'd probably find even more evidence, and she didn't want to witness the look in his eyes when he did.

Her breath caught in her throat. Would he turn his back on her when he was convinced she was a killer? How could she find Brittany without his help?

She held tight to the memories of their lovemaking, hoping they would be enough to last a lifetime that might stretch to endless years in prison—or end quickly in the state's electric chair. Soon, when he discovered proof of her crime, her memories might be all of him she'd have left.

"Why do I have to come with you?" she asked for the third time, wanting to stall his entry into the house. "I don't know anything about investigating."

The determined look in his eyes gentled. "Afraid to go inside?"

She squinted in the morning sun. "Scared stiff."

"Swinburn's dead. He can't hurt you."

"It's not David I'm afraid of." She couldn't tell Jordan she was afraid of losing him.

"There's no one else there."

"Please—"

"Your fear could be a good sign."

She shook her head, aware he'd misunderstood but reluctant to set him straight. "Nothing good about being afraid."

He returned to the lower level, cupped her elbow and steered her toward the entrance nearest the pool. "Let's get this over with."

They skirted the tiled edge of the pool, whose blue-green waters shimmered in the sunlight, and stepped into the shade of the cloistered walk that ran along the west side of the house.

"Fiona said the far left entry opens into Swinburn's study," he said, "where the body was found."

He opened the door and stepped inside a luxurious bathroom. "This isn't the study. I must have misunderstood Fiona."

Angel glanced around the room. A sudden wave of dizziness washed over her, and she clutched clumsily at the marble vanity to keep from falling.

"Easy." Jordan slipped his arm around her. "Don't pass out on me."

"Please, get me out of here."

He led her back to a shaded lounge chair beside the pool, and she lay back and closed her eyes while Jordan rubbed her icy hands.

"You've gone white as a sheet." Worry laced his usually steady voice. "I'll get Henry to take us to Emergency."

She grabbed his hands and opened her eyes. "You understood Fiona perfectly."

Confusion joined the worry on his face. "What are you talking about?"

"That bathroom—" she nodded toward the door they'd just exited "—leads directly into David's study."

His eyes widened in surprise. "You remember?"

She nodded, shaken by a jumble of terror and relief. "I remember...*everything*."

Chapter Nine

"You remember *everything?*" Jordan sank beside her on the lounge chair.

She trembled at remembered fear, but hope buoyed her. "Stepping into that room brought it all back."

"David—"

"I didn't kill him."

His tanned face settled into grim lines. "According to the state attorney's evidence, we'll have a hard time proving it. You'd better tell me what happened. Don't leave out even the smallest detail."

She shifted upright in the chair, drew a deep breath and forced herself to recall the horror. "It all began four days ago...."

LATE SUNDAY AFTERNOON on the street outside David's estate, she had opened the glove compartment of her red Nissan and reached for the revolver hidden beneath a jumble of road maps. Her hand shook so violently, she jerked it out and pressed it against her thudding heart.

She saw her reflection before she squeezed her

eyes tight—lips compressed, cheeks drained of color, hair tousled and eyes wide with fright, staring back at her from the rearview mirror like some crazed stranger.

I'll make *you tell where you've hidden Brittany,* she had threatened David over the phone earlier, *even if I have to* kill *you.*

She'd been bluffing, of course. As hatefully as David had treated her—lying, cheating and now abducting two-year-old Brittany from her custody—she could never pull the trigger. He was her daughter's father, after all, and Sara had once loved him. At least, she'd loved the image of the man she'd believed him to be.

But David didn't know she wouldn't kill him. In his ignorance, she might force him to reveal where he'd taken Brittany. Her grim determination to recover her daughter infused her with new courage. She grabbed the gun and shoved it into her purse.

Stepping onto the street, she glanced around. She had parked beneath a Chinese banyan whose high, spreading branches filtered the heat of the late afternoon sun. No one could see her. High walls surrounded every estate in the Sunset Bay waterfront neighborhood where David had brought her to live after their marriage three years ago, and, at the moment, no traffic circulated on the exclusive streets.

With an unsteady hand, she smoothed a nonexistent wrinkle from her white linen suit, one of two outfits she'd kept from the vast wardrobe David had selected for her. His insistence on choosing her clothes had been the first sign of trouble in their brief marriage.

His taste had been expensive and impeccable, but it wasn't hers. Unaccustomed to wealth or pretension, she preferred casual blouses and skirts or jeans and sneakers, but David had pitched a fit if she wore her own choices and demanded she change into what he had bought her. Today, not wanting anything to distract him from her purpose, she had dressed to his specifications.

Slinging the strap of her purse over her shoulder, she felt the weight of the gun against her hip as she walked quickly to the ironwork gate at the rear of the property. An unnatural stillness filled the air, like an unsettling calm before a storm, and the *tip-tap* of her low-heeled sandals on the brick walkway clicked loudly in the silence.

She stopped before the rear gate, where a touch pad, mounted on the wall beside the entry, winked red. At the sight of the armed alarm, her heart sank like a brick in a pond, and she slumped against the ivy-covered wall. She had forgotten the high-tech security system David had installed shortly before their marriage had begun to deteriorate.

How could she threaten him if she couldn't reach him?

Oh, Brittany.

Tears blurred her vision. She ached to hold her daughter, to twine her fingers in the silky smoothness of her blond curls, to watch her hazel eyes sparkle when she giggled, to hear the happy babble of her voice.

Yesterday David had called and in a cold, bitter voice announced that he wouldn't return Brittany after his weekly, court-ordered outing. With a cruel laugh, he claimed he'd sent Brittany away, where Sara would never find her.

Frantic, she had called Fiona. The housekeeper had sadly confirmed her daughter wasn't at David's, that he had taken the child away that morning and returned without her.

After hanging up from her conversation with Fiona, she had called the Sunset Bay police. "My daughter's been abducted."

"Hold on, ma'am. I'll transfer you to a detective."

She had paced the floor of her living room until a man on the other end of the line identified himself as Detective Rick Panowski.

"Do you know who took your daughter, Mrs. Swinburn?" was the first question he asked.

"My ex-husband."

"And you have sole custody?"

"He has weekend visitation rights."

"Today's Saturday," Panowski said, as if she were an idiot who didn't know what day it was.

"My husband called and told me not to pick up Brittany tomorrow, that he's hidden her where I can't find her." Sara bit back tears. "She's only two. She won't understand why her mother doesn't come for her."

"Is your ex the type who might hurt the child?"

"Of course not!"

Panowski sighed. "I'm afraid we can't treat this as a priority, since it's a parental abduction and not a violent crime."

Sara went numb with surprise. "But he's breaking the law. The court gave *me* custody of my daughter."

"What you need to do is call your lawyer."

"But my baby—"

"Come down to the station and fill out a report, Mrs. Swinburn, but I can't make any promises."

She slammed the receiver, sickened by the knowledge the police wouldn't help her. Her only consolation was knowing David wouldn't allow anyone to harm or frighten Brittany. He loved his daughter passionately, almost as intensely as he hated his ex-wife.

Saturday night, during the small hours of the morning when worry and outrage had kept her awake, she devised her plan. Now, choked with anger, she considered the touch pad that separated her from David—and her daughter.

How could he call himself a father when he'd stolen their child not for himself, but to hide her from her mother, just for spite?

Fury fueled her courage. As if pummeling David himself, she punched in the numbers of the old code, the only one she knew, and held her breath. An electronic signal hummed, and she tensed, anticipating piercing shrieks from sirens mounted under the eaves of the Mediterranean-style mansion.

No alarm sounded. Quietly, the gate's lock clicked.

Weak with relief, she squared her shoulders, pushed open the gate and stepped onto the grounds. Her gaze swept the four-car garage with the Erskines' apartment above, the greenhouse beyond where David grew his prized orchids, the spacious terrace surrounding the pool and the dock on Sunset Bay.

Not another soul in sight.

Kneeling beside a landscaped border that edged the brick path, she selected a fist-size river rock, then returned to the entry and jammed it between the gate and wall. If she needed to make a speedy retreat, she wouldn't have to stop to activate the touch pad.

An arbor of confederate jasmine screened the path from the house, and she hurried along the cool, shadowed walk to the rear door. When she had lived here, Fiona and Henry had always taken Sundays off, and, as usual, the kitchen was deserted. She hurried past stainless steel appliances and counters backed with hand-painted tiles and pushed through a swinging door into the hall that led to the study.

A creature of habit, David always spent Sunday afternoons there bringing the household records up-to-date.

A rapid check of the spacious formal rooms on the first floor revealed no signs of any occupants, and she returned to the heavy paneled door of the study and drew the revolver from her purse.

With her heart hammering in her throat and perspiration slicking her palm, she gripped the butt tight to still her trembling hand, twisted the antique brass handle and stepped inside.

David wasn't there.

Her knees buckled with a combination of disappointment and relief. Then she spotted the computer on the credenza behind his desk. Its lighted screen held the first page of David's personal financial program. She rushed across the room, laid her gun beside the computer and hit the page down key. If she could find a record of David's payment for Brittany's care, she could locate her daughter without an ugly confrontation.

Scanning quickly, she flipped through page after page, searching for an unfamiliar name among the household's employees and suppliers. On page twelve, the notation jumped out at her: *Carleton James. Paid. Fifty thousand dollars.*

Who was Carleton James? Could David have hired him to care for Brittany? She made a mental note of the name but doubted James was the baby-sitter. As much as David doted on Brittany, he loved money more. He would never have paid such a ridiculous sum for his daughter's care.

She called up the next page, and a muffled noise reverberated in the hall. David was coming downstairs.

With lightning speed, she leapt from the chair and scrambled around the enormous mahogany desk into the adjoining bathroom. Its door clicked behind her as the study door opened.

Too late, she realized she'd forgotten her gun.

Laying her head against the door frame, she muffled a groan. David would spot the revolver and know she'd been there. The first month of their marriage, over her strident protests, he'd insisted on buying her that particular weapon to carry in her car.

Without her gun, she had no bargaining power to force him to reveal Brittany's whereabouts.

Intending to slip away unnoticed, she tiptoed across the room to the outer door that led to the pool. At the sound of a strange voice in the study, she halted. Stealing back to the closed door, she placed her ear against the panels, hoping the stranger might be the person David had placed in charge of Brittany.

"Just keep moving, Swinburn," the deep, menacing voice demanded, "with your hands up."

"And don't try nothing stupid," another masculine voice added, "'cause unless we leave here with the money you owe, you're a dead man."

Terrified by the ruthlessness in their voices, she froze. If she bolted, they might hear and come after her.

"Gentlemen, be reasonable." David's smooth, cultivated voice, that she'd once found so appealing, held a hard edge of panic. "I intend to pay. I just can't do it today."

"Like you couldn't last week, and the week before, and the week before that?" the first voice asked with a sarcastic snarl.

"I explained to C.J.—"

C.J. Carleton James?

"You're trying my patience," the stranger continued. "You almost blew the cover on our entire scheme last year. We had to waste those undercover cops to save your worthless hide and keep our operation afloat. But were you grateful? No, you're not even paying your IOUs."

"Yeah," the second man said, "and that lady cop's death brought down major heat. No thanks to you, we managed to keep our operation under wraps. Unfortunately, her partner survived. At first, he was too weak or too polluted to cause trouble. Now word on the street is he's sobered up. And he's sharp. Once he starts putting two and two together, he'll figure out *you're* involved."

"Could be he's already made the connection," the first man said. "Has Jordan Trouble been snooping around?"

David laughed his superior laugh, the one that had always made her feel two inches tall. "Jordan Trouble? The only trouble I've had is you two. I told you I'd pay, and I will, but when I'm damned good and ready. I don't respond to threats. Now get the hell out of my house and leave me alone."

"Stop right there," the first man ordered sharply, "and back away from that table."

"Well, well," the second said in a surprised tone, "what have we here? You weren't planning to shoot us, were you, Swinburn?"

They had discovered her gun.

"Believe me, I didn't know the gun was there." David's superior tone had vanished and frantic pleading replaced it. "That's my ex-wife's gun. She must be here in the house somewhere."

"No matter," the first man said with a growl that sent chills down her back. "We'll find her. When we're through with you."

The second man chuckled. "Like we said, Swinburn, we're clean out of patience. And we figure if Jordan Trouble gets his hands on you, you'll squeal like a stuck pig to save your own miserable hide."

"I won't! I swear it!"

"Too late," the first voice said coldly. "You've become a major liability."

"*Sayonara,* Swinburn," the other said.

"No, please!" David shrieked.

A shot rang out. Then another. And a third.

She cupped her ears and suppressed a scream. The thunder of blood in her head almost drowned out the crack of three more shots.

"Now," a gruff voice said, "let's find the woman."

The words jolted her from her paralysis. She lurched to the pool door, unfastened the dead bolt with clumsy fingers and fled across the pool deck to the path beneath the arbor.

Angry shouts and the thud of running feet had followed her.

EXHAUSTED, Angel collapsed against the chair. "So you see, *I* didn't kill David. Frank and Sidney did."

She couldn't judge from Jordan's impassive expression whether he believed her. When she had related Frank and Sidney's account of killing his partner, his face had darkened with a frightening rage, and he had bounded from the chair to prowl the pool deck. By the time she'd finished her story, he had resumed his seat and the familiar, amiable mask that hid his true feelings.

"If I hadn't left the rear gate propped open," she said, "they would have caught me when I ran."

"How did they end up with your car?"

"I dropped my purse. Without car keys, I couldn't use the Nissan to escape, so I ducked through an open gate next door, cut across the lawn to the bay and waded through the water back here. I climbed the stairs outside the garage and hid on the Erskines' porch until after dark."

"You didn't hear Frank and Sidney leave?"

"For all I knew, they were still on the grounds looking for me. I didn't dare go back into the house."

"Not even to call an ambulance?"

His neutral voice held no accusation, but she squirmed with guilt just the same, wondering if she might have saved David. "I counted six shots and doubted he had survived. And I had Brittany to consider. Who would raise my child if we'd both been killed?"

"And once it turned dark?"

"Between worry over Brittany and terror at the attack on David, I wasn't thinking straight. All I wanted was my daughter. I started walking, a two-hour hike from here to my ex-in-laws on Turtle Key. While they slept, I forced my way into their house, hoping I'd find Brittany.''

''But she wasn't there.''

She shook her head, unable to face him.

''Why didn't you call the police first?''

''Hindsight says I should have, but that night I was paranoid and almost in shock. The day before, Panowski had refused to search for Brittany, and I couldn't imagine him believing my story of David's shooting. Frank and Sidney had framed me, using my gun to murder David. I was afraid I'd never find my daughter if I went to jail.''

''So you came looking for me.''

She lifted her eyes and met his gaze. His expression was unreadable, but he had tensed like a tightly coiled spring. She expected him to resume pacing any moment.

''Frank and Sidney mentioned you,'' she explained. ''I hoped you would help me find Brittany.''

''You heard Frank and Sidney say where to find me?''

She shook her head. ''I called the Sunset Bay police station from the extension in George Swinburn's study, pretending to be your cousin from up north, and asked how to locate you. The desk sergeant suggested Mary Tiger's bar. But I can't figure out how Frank and Sidney followed me there.''

A cold, deadly calm settled over Jordan. ''You were just an added bonus.''

She frowned, puzzled as much by his demeanor as his words. "I don't understand."

"They came to Mary Tiger's looking for me. When they discovered you there, too, they must have figured you a more immediate threat and tried to take you with them."

"You never saw them before Sunday night?"

He shook his head.

"Not even the night they shot you?"

He didn't answer, but stared across the terrace to the gulf, his face devoid of emotion, his eyes cold and empty. His body radiated heat, but his wounded soul seemed miles away.

She placed her hand on his arm, longing to restore the warmth she'd seen in his eyes last night when they'd made love. "So Frank and Sidney went to Mary Tiger's, intending to kill you, and found me instead?"

He turned to face her with the glazed look of someone awakening suddenly from deep sleep. "It all makes sense now. David was handling monies from the real estate scam Carleton James had masterminded. Your ex was murdered for not turning over the profits—and so he wouldn't reveal James's part in the fraud."

Despite the warm morning sun, she shivered. David had tried to control his partner in crime with the same ruthlessness he'd used to hide Brittany from her, but he'd underestimated James and paid the ultimate price. Now *she* was a threat to the man who ordered others' deaths so casually. "Frank and Sidney want me dead so I can't identify them as David's killers.''

''They won't kill you until you've told them what they want to know.''

The implications made her hands shake. ''They want the money David took. But I have no idea where it is.''

He closed his hand over hers still gripping his arm. ''Frank and Sidney wiped the hard drive after searching for the money's location in David's computer. If they had found where the profits were stashed, they wouldn't be looking for Brittany now to force you to talk.''

''Brittany...'' Her throat closed with panic.

''Finding her won't be easy without David's financial files to point us in the right direction.''

Another memory, clear and crisp, shot into her consciousness. Breaking from his grasp, she jumped from the lounge chair. ''Follow me.''

She darted into the bathroom off the pool, rushed through David's study and took the wide, curving stairs two at a time. Jordan sprinted behind her. At the end of the long upstairs hall, she flung open the door to David's dressing room. With a protectiveness that brought a lump to her throat, Jordan pulled her aside and entered first.

''You don't expect Frank and Sidney to show up here?'' she said as he checked closets and the adjoining bathroom. ''Not with police crawling all over the place?''

''The cops are gone now, and Frank and Sidney

may come back looking for what they couldn't find before.''

''I *hope* they didn't find it.''

She edged past him into the room, dropped to her hands and knees and crawled into the kneehole beneath the vanity. She pried the beige carpeting away from the wall.

Jordan squeezed into the opening, his face inches from hers, his broad shoulders filling the remaining space. ''Mind if I ask what you're doing?''

''Floor safe.'' She spun the numbered dial in the gray steel door embedded in the floorboards. His breath warmed her cheek, scattering her thoughts as she struggled to remember the combination.

''Swinburn didn't switch the combination when you moved out?''

''I doubt it. David didn't like changes. He had a terrible memory, so keeping the same numbers made things easier for him.'' That fact triggered the information she needed. ''The alarm system, his voice mail, his computer password and safe combination—he used the same code for all of them, 2-8-59, his birth date.''

Jordan's lips quirked in an ironic grin. ''Made things easier for burglars and computer hackers, too.''

''We'll know in a minute if he was true to his habits.'' She twisted the dial to the right.

Exhaling a sigh of relief when the tumblers finally aligned, she swung open the safe's door and spotted a large manila envelope.

"This is it!" She grabbed the package and scooted from beneath the vanity, forcing Jordan out with her. Scrambling to her feet, she displayed her find.

"James's money?"

"Better."

She wheeled, raced downstairs to David's study and dropped into his leather-covered desk chair. With nervous fingers, she unwound the red string that secured the flap of the envelope and reached inside. Her hand closed around the object she hoped would lead her to her baby.

Kneeling beside her, Jordan frowned at the disc she waved beneath his nose. "A disc? Of what?"

With a push of her toes, she rolled the chair to the computer table behind the desk and slid the disc into the backup drive. "David was a fanatic about backing up his files, ever since a couple years ago when he lost everything to a power surge. If I can restore his financial program, maybe I can figure out where he took Brittany."

A dangerous stillness settled over Jordan. He stood and dipped his hands into the back pockets of his jeans, but the casual movement didn't hide his tension. "I need proof to nail Carleton James's hide to the wall. I hope it's there."

The rancor in his voice frightened her, and the sharp, craggy angles of his face were as rigid as quarried stone.

"Convicting James is that important to you?"

"As important as finding Brittany is to you."

She was struck again by how little she knew about

Jordan. He had never mentioned his female partner, the one who had died in the undercover operation when he'd been shot and left for dead. She wondered if his resolve to see James pay for his crimes sprang from Jordan's innate sense of justice or from the deeper wounds of anger and pain he tried to hide beneath his cavalier manner.

Had he loved the woman Carleton James had ordered killed?

Last night, Jordan had held her, comforted her and made love to her with a passion and intensity she'd never known. But he hadn't said he loved her. Did his heart belong to the partner he'd buried a year ago?

Sadness washed over her. She no longer worried that he wouldn't love her because she was a murderer. The return of her memories had erased that fear. Instead, she faced a daunting rival, his dead partner.

How can I compete with a ghost?

"It won't load itself," Jordan said.

Roused from her musings, she blinked. "Sorry?"

"The computer won't load itself."

"Right." Embarrassed that he'd caught her woolgathering, she turned back to the backup drive and began to reinstall David's personal finance program.

While the program loaded, she pondered her daughter's disappearance. "Why hasn't whoever has Brittany come forward with her? With all the media coverage, the sitter must know she's the child the police are looking for."

Jordan pulled his hands from his pockets and propped his hips on the edge of the desk. "If *you* wanted to hide Brittany from someone, what would you do?"

"I'd take her as far away as possible, so that person could never find her." She shuddered. Frank and Sidney, as well as the police, were searching for her daughter.

"What if you wanted to spend time with her while she's in hiding?"

"If I took her somewhere close enough that I could visit her, I'd run the risk of others finding her." Puzzled, she plumbed the depths of his blue-black eyes. "But David took her within a hundred miles of here." Her blood ran suddenly cold. "Unless he put her on a plane last Saturday."

He shook his head. "The authorities checked all the airports when they were searching for you. Airline personnel would have remembered a cute kid like Brittany."

"Maybe the sitter is afraid to come forward."

"Could be. But I think her not knowing the child in her care is Brittany Swinburn is a better possibility." He lifted his eyebrow, the one with several tiny stitches, reminders that she owed him her life for fighting off Frank and Sidney that night at Mary Tiger's.

"You think David gave the sitter a false name?"

Jordan nodded. "And paid her in cash or by cashier's check in order to hide his identity."

"That would explain why the sitter hasn't made a

connection between Brittany and the missing child on the news.''

"Let's hope David had time to record that payment before he was killed.''

The hum of the backup drive ended, and she swiveled toward the computer with her heart in her throat. "We're about to find out.''

Scrolling to the latest entry, dated the day of David's murder, she worked her way backward through the program. Jordan read over her shoulder, scribbling furiously on a pad he'd removed from the desk each time Carleton James's name appeared.

She flipped through four weeks' entries without a single unidentifiable name. Her hope was slipping, edged aside by anxiety, as she paged to the next entry.

"That's it!'' Jordan smacked the monitor with the palm of his hand. "Helen Murtaugh, Fort Myers. Paid five thousand dollars for the month of April.''

She stared at the name, afraid to get her hopes up again.

"Remember what Henry said?'' Jordan asked. "Fort Myers is within a hundred-mile radius, and it's where the Department of Agriculture was spraying for medflies last Saturday when David took Brittany in the car.''

She shut down the computer and pushed to her feet. "Let's go.''

Waving the pad he'd filled with figures, Jordan didn't accompany her. "Maggie Henderson should have these notes on Carleton James.''

"I'm going to Fort Myers."

"You can't go alone."

"I have to find my baby."

"And what about Frank and Sidney?"

"I'm in disguise. Besides, they won't be looking for me in Fort Myers."

"Not unless they made copies of these financial programs before they erased the hard drive and contact Murtaugh themselves. They stumbled across your trail once before, remember?"

"I can't leave Brittany." She pivoted and rushed through the study bathroom to the pool deck.

He caught up with her, grabbed her arm and swung her to face him. "I *have* to contact the police first. James has to be stopped. Both Jenny and Swinburn are dead because of him."

"Jenny?"

"My partner." His expression couldn't have been more anguished if she'd twisted a knife in his heart. "I owe it to her to bring James down."

She jerked free. "I have an obligation to my daughter."

She hurried along the path to the Erskines' apartment in search of Henry. She'd ask him to lend her his car.

Jordan called after her. "Jenny—"

"Jenny's *dead*," she whirled and shouted, tormented by anxiety for Brittany. "Brittany's alive. I have to find her."

She turned her back on him again, darted across

the cobbled courtyard and ran head-on into Fiona at the foot of the stairs.

The housekeeper grabbed her to keep her from falling. "Miz Sara! You look like the devil himself's nipping at your heels."

"Where's Henry?"

Fiona jerked her chin upward. "Finishing his tea. Is something wrong?"

"I need a car."

Fiona folded her hands at her waist and assumed her mother-hen look, a familiar expression now that Angel's memory had returned. "Have you had breakfast?"

"No time. I—"

"Without proper nourishment, you willna have the strength to help your wee lass." Fiona tucked Angel's arm beneath her elbow and led her upstairs.

Drinking from a mammoth teacup and reading the paper, Henry sat in his shirtsleeves and suspenders on the open porch. "Morning, Miz Sara."

"I need your car, Henry."

"Not before she's had a proper breakfast," Fiona ordered. "Now sit you down, and I'll bring you a bite."

The housekeeper pointed to a chair. Angel looked to Henry for help, but he merely shrugged. Recognizing the futility of arguing with a Scottish brick wall, she sat. Fiona gave a satisfied nod and went inside.

Henry drained the last of his tea and smiled.

"Might as well do as she says. Takes less time in the long run."

"Brittany's in Fort Myers. May I use your car to bring her back?"

He stood, unrolled his sleeves and buttoned the cuffs. "It'll need petrol if you're going that far, but filling it won't take long. I'll be back before you've finished breakfast."

His footsteps rattled down the stairs, and she was about to rise and follow, when Fiona shoved open the screen door from the apartment.

"This'll fill the hollows in those cheeks, lass." The housekeeper placed a tray on the table beside Angel's chair and poured two cups of tea. "Wouldna mind another cup myself. I can keep you company while you eat. Where's your nice young man?"

"He had other business to take care of."

Fiona handed her a cup of steaming tea, took one for herself and settled on the opposite chair. The white wicker creaked beneath her weight, and she studied Angel with periwinkle-blue eyes. "He's smitten with you, you know."

Angel shook her head.

Fiona bobbed her head, bouncing her white curls. "I know what I saw. Even my Henry, who's usually blind to such things, noticed. Jordan Trouble looks at you like a starving man contemplates a banquet. And he calls you *Angel*."

With a start, she realized, even with her memories restored, she no longer thought of herself as Sara. She had closed the door on that chapter of her life.

Fiona leaned toward her and patted her hand. "Drink your tea, Miz Sara. Henry's bringing the car, and things will work out."

Her throat tight with worry over Brittany, Angel doubted she could swallow, but she sipped the hot beverage and nibbled at Fiona's hot scones.

Angel set down her cup when the crunch of tires in the courtyard signaled Henry's return.

"More tea?" Fiona asked.

She shook her head and stood. "The car's here. Thanks for breakfast."

Before Fiona could snare her again, she escaped down the stairs, skidded around the back of the car and pulled up short in surprise.

Jordan waited, leaning against the passenger door of the Lincoln. She hadn't thought it possible, but he looked more attractive than ever with sunlight bathing the rugged lines of his face through the dappled shade of the banyans. His polo shirt accented the muscular contours of his shoulders and chest, and his blue-black eyes impaled her with an intensity that made her squirm.

"Your car, madam," he said in an imitation of Henry's English accent.

Stunned, she managed to draw enough breath to ask, "Where's Henry?"

"Inventorying the silver for the estate." Jordan opened the door. "We're wasting time."

Eager to find Brittany and elated at Jordan's return, she didn't argue. She scooted onto the seat, and he circled the car and climbed behind the wheel.

"You were going to the police station," she said.

He nodded, turned the ignition and started the limousine down the drive toward the tall gates, that swung open at their approach.

"If the station's where you're headed, you can let me out now."

"I used David's fax to send my notes on Carleton James to Maggie." He dug into his shirt pocket and handed her a folded sheet of paper.

After the disastrous events of the past few days, she expected unpleasant news when she opened it. Instead, she found Helen Murtaugh's address scrawled in Jordan's bold handwriting.

"Where did you find this?"

"Library. Handy things. You should try one sometime." His cavalier mask fit seamlessly, concealing all other emotions.

"You didn't have time to visit a library."

"Right, but I called the Fort Myers Library reference desk instead. According to their city directory, Helen Murtaugh is a retired preschool teacher."

"Shouldn't we call her? Tell her we're coming?"

"We don't know her involvement in David's scheme. She may try to hide Brittany. Better catch her by surprise."

With Helen Murtaugh's address in hand and the Lincoln speeding through the city toward the interstate, she allowed herself to anticipate a reunion with her child. With a sigh of contentment, she leaned back in her seat, feeling as if a load of stones had been shifted from her shoulders.

The only hitch in her happiness was the enigmatic man beside her. She had grown to care too much for him, a man with too many secrets, a man who held too much of himself in reserve.

She'd made a mistake when she'd married David, accepting him at face value. Too late she'd learned of the controlling, obsessive personality he'd hidden beneath his suave and cultured demeanor.

Jordan lacked the unpleasant characteristics she'd noted in David soon after her marriage. But she'd caught occasional glimpses of Jordan's wounded soul in the depths of his eyes and seen flashes of deep sorrow before he'd hidden it behind his devil-may-care grin.

Even if she proved her innocence in David's murder, she had no future with Jordan, a man anchored in the past, haunted by the ghost of the woman he loved.

The impossibility of a life with Jordan saddened her, but she refused to allow her melancholy to blunt the joy of her reunion with Brittany. Precious memories of her daughter made her smile, and she clutched those images fiercely, drawing comfort from them during the two-hour trip through monotonous stretches of pines and palmettos.

When Jordan exited the interstate into Fort Myers, her anticipation mushroomed. Within minutes, he located the quiet street and parked the car in front of an apartment building set in a neatly trimmed lawn of saint augustine grass and shaded by royal palms and poinciana trees aflame with lacy orange blossoms.

Before he could turn off the engine, she leapt out of the car and ran up the walkway to Murtaugh's apartment on the bottom floor. Anxious to hold her baby and anticipating Brittany's delight at seeing her, she rang the bell.

No one answered.

Jordan came up behind her, and she rang the bell again.

"Maybe Mrs. Murtaugh's out," he said.

A wiry, gray-haired man carrying a shuffleboard cue came out of the apartment next door. He stopped when he spotted them. "You folks looking for Helen?"

"Do you know where she is?" Angel asked.

"Gone," he said. "She and the girl—cute little tyke—moved out three days ago."

Chapter Ten

At Angel's horrified reaction, Jordan slipped quickly into his former role as investigator. "Did Helen have any close friends here in the complex?"

"Her and Inez were buddies. Went everywhere together." The old man nodded toward the corner apartment, then scurried away toward the shuffleboard courts visible behind the building.

Angel met Jordan's gaze with bleak eyes. "What if—"

"Don't torture yourself." He shot her an encouraging smile and guided her toward the corner unit. "Let's see what Inez can tell us."

A few minutes later they were back in the car, following Inez's carefully drawn map to a subdivision halfway between the city and Sanibel Island.

The traffic thinned, and Jordan glanced at Angel from the corner of his eye. She sat ramrod stiff, her hands strangling the shoulder harness, her face drawn and pale. Overwhelming love and a zealous desire to protect her from all hurt vibrated through him, awakening his fears and amplifying his inadequacies. He had despised his own company for the past year yet had somehow survived. But if anything happened to Angel or Brittany, if he failed them as he had failed Jenny, he wouldn't be able to live with himself.

Reaching across the wide front seat, he ran his knuckle down her cheek and felt her shiver beneath his touch. "Relax. We know Brittany's there, and Inez telephoned Mrs. Murtaugh and told her we're on our way."

She turned, and tears muddied the brown of her eyes. "I'm scared."

"That she won't know you? You haven't been apart that long."

"How can I keep her safe with hired killers after us?"

His vow to protect them died on his tongue. *Never promise what you can't deliver.* Frustrated at his inability to ease her apprehension, he squeezed her shoulder and returned his hand to the wheel. "There's only one solution."

"James and his killers must be caught." She wiped her tears with the back of her hand and stiffened her spine. "This nightmare can't go on forever."

He wanted to contradict her but couldn't. His nightmare had lasted over a year, with no end in sight.

Twenty minutes after leaving the apartment complex, he pulled the Lincoln alongside the curb at the address Inez had given them and killed the motor.

Helen Murtaugh's new home was a quaint little

bungalow surrounded by a white picket fence almost hidden by yellow bougainvillea. The front door opened, and a woman with a remarkable resemblance to Fiona stepped onto the porch. In her arms, she held a sweet-faced toddler with golden Shirley Temple curls.

With a joyful cry, Angel bounded from the car and sprinted toward the house.

The woman set the child on her feet, and Brittany tottered toward Angel on pudgy legs.

"Mommy! Mommy!"

Angel scooped up the girl and clasped her tightly. When Jordan reached them, she was murmuring, "Mommy's come to take you home, sweetheart."

He swallowed hard against the tightness in his throat at the picture they made—Angel, her face wet with tears, and Brittany, her tiny hands gently patting her mother's damp cheeks.

"Brittany," Mrs. Murtaugh said, "take your mommy around back and show her your playhouse while I talk with Mr. Trouble."

Brittany squirmed, and Angel set her on her feet.

"'Mon, Mommy. See."

As if suddenly remembering he was there, Angel sent him a questioning look.

"It's okay," he said. "I'll explain everything to Mrs. Murtaugh."

Angel's honey-maple eyes sparkled with happiness, and the beauty of the smile she bestowed on him made him struggle for breath. Her look communicated much more than the joy of her reunion with her daughter.

He forced himself to turn away. He couldn't accept the love she'd offered him, the promises her eyes pledged. He was too broken, too scarred, and Angel deserved better.

"Sit here, Mr. Trouble." Mrs. Murtaugh patted the glider seat next to her.

Jordan climbed onto the porch, sat beside her and handed her the custody documents he and Angel had picked up at Angel's apartment on their way out of Sunset Bay.

Mrs. Murtaugh studied them through her bifocals, then raised her head. "I never made a connection between the murdered man on the news and Brittany's father."

"If you need to call the police to verify—"

"That won't be necessary. Brittany's delight at seeing her mother is all the proof I need."

"Then taking Brittany with us won't be a problem?"

She dabbed at her forehead, moist from the heat, with a lace-edged handkerchief. "It's such a shock. Mr. David—or I should say Mr. Swinburn—told me Brittany's mother had died. And now he's dead himself, poor man."

Jordan kept his opinion of David Swinburn to himself. "If you'll show me Brittany's things, I'll load them in the car."

By the time Angel and Brittany returned to the front of the house, he had packed Brittany's luggage

and secured the child carrier in the back seat. After
Mrs. Murtaugh's tearful goodbye—she'd obviously
adored the little girl—Angel climbed into the back
seat next to Brittany and he headed for home.

Just a few minutes north of Fort Myers, he glanced
into the rearview mirror. Angel was watching her
sleeping daughter as if afraid Brittany would disappear if she looked away.

He pulled his gaze back to the interstate. The muscles of his neck and shoulders ached from his state
of constant alert, and the return to Sunset Bay meant
even greater vigilance. Frank and Sidney were looking for them, and it was up to Jordan to keep Angel
and Brittany beyond the killers' reach.

ALTHOUGH THE SUN HAD SET an hour earlier, Jordan
wore his dark glasses until he'd slipped into the rear
booth of the diner, across from Maggie Henderson.
Dressed in fitted jeans and a tweed blazer, the petite
detective with her red hair blazing in the soft light
looked deceptively fragile, alone on the padded
bench.

He grinned. Maggie's illusory delicacy had caused
the downfall of many a lawbreaker. He'd witnessed
her sending a two-hundred-and-fifty-pound drunk
and disorderly truck driver to his knees through the
skilled use of pressure points, right before she
slapped the cuffs on him. Wanted for assault and
battery on his girlfriend, the trucker never knew what
hit him. The guys at the station called her Mighty

Mouse—behind her back. No one had the guts to say it to her face.

"You alone?" he asked.

She narrowed eyes as brilliantly blue as an October sky. "Why all the secrecy?"

"Remember the fraud case I was working last year?"

Sadness etched her heart-shaped features. "Wish I could forget."

"I have a new lead."

"Yeah, Carleton James, according to your fax. Panowski caught the fraud case after you. Shouldn't you be talking to him?"

"The fraud case is connected to the Swinburn murder."

"You're sure?"

Jordan waited while a teenage waitress poured coffee and took their order before launching into his story of everything that had happened from the night Angel walked into his life.

Later, when he'd related Frank's comments about James's mole in the police department, Maggie shoved aside the slice of pie and wiped her fingers. "Everyone in CID has worked together for years. Are you sure you heard right?"

"How else can you explain Spacek showing up at the hearing and agreeing to post such a ridiculous bail?"

She wrinkled her freckled nose thoughtfully. "A departmental spy would also explain how the scam artists knew you and Jenny were cops that night last April.''

''That's why I asked to see you alone, Mags. You're the only one I can trust.''

She eyed him keenly. ''And you're not that sure of me, are you?''

He shrugged. ''At this point, I have no choice. I have to trust someone, because I need help.'' He finished his story, describing Angel's account of Swinburn's murder, and dug into the pocket of his windbreaker. ''Here's a copy of the backup disc of Swinburn's computer files. It contains the information about James I faxed you this morning.''

She took the disc and slid it into her blazer pocket. ''This is a start, but not enough for a conviction.''

''I'm hoping you'll find the evidence you need here.'' He dangled a small key across the table. ''This was in the envelope with the disc.''

She took the key and turned it over in her small hand. ''To a safety deposit box?''

''Swinburn's. You're the lead investigator in his homicide, so you should have no trouble gaining access.'' He scribbled his cell phone number on a napkin and pushed it across the table. ''In case you need to contact me.''

Her sky-blue eyes locked with his. ''I want you to back off the case. If this James was Jenny's killer, there's no way you can be objective.''

He met her gaze without flinching. If James had been responsible for Jenny's death, it would take more than Mighty Mouse Henderson to keep him away. "I've found the Swinburn kid, so you can call off the search."

"Where is she?"

"Safe, with her mother." He reached for the bill, but Maggie beat him to it.

"This one's on the department. And, Trouble?"

"Yeah."

"Watch your back."

While Maggie paid the tab, Jordan pushed through the glass doors and walked a full circuit of the parking lot, scanning the cars, before mounting Henry's cycle and roaring off.

SITTING ON THE BENCH in the cabin cruiser's stern, Angel clasped her knees against her chest and watched the evening star slide toward the western gulf. Only hours ago, after Jordan returned from meeting Detective Henderson, Angel had kissed Brittany goodbye.

Fiona and Henry had driven away with her daughter, waving happily from her carrier in the back seat of their ancient Chevy. As much as Angel hated another separation, she'd had to admit Brittany's safety was more important than her mother's desire to keep her close.

"Two weeks ago," Fiona had said when Angel and Jordan returned from Fort Myers, "Mr. Swinburn sent Henry and me to Orlando to clean and stock his new condo near Sea World. I suspect he meant to spend weekends there with the wee lass, well out of your sight."

"If you like," Henry said, "we can take Brittany there until the difficulty here is sorted out."

"And those dreadful men are behind bars," Fiona added.

The Erskines' suggestion had been an answer to a prayer. The couple had been surrogate grandparents to Brittany since the day she was born, Sea World was her favorite place, and, since ownership of the condo was listed under an obscure corporation name, Frank and Sidney wouldn't know to look for her there.

Angel hugged her knees tighter, longing for Brittany. Her daughter's absence ached like an unhealed wound, but at least her child was safe and happy and knew her mother would be coming for her soon.

"It's not too late." Jordan interrupted her musings.

Angel glanced over her shoulder toward land, where Sunset Bay's lights illuminated low clouds in the eastern sky. "It's almost midnight."

He sank beside her, pulled her back against his chest and wrapped his arms around her. "It's not too late for you to join Brittany in Orlando."

"Not until the men who're after us are caught. I can't risk leading them to her."

"Taking you to Orlando without them picking up your trail would be easy." His breath warmed the back of her neck.

"If I can't prove my innocence, I'll go to prison and be separated from Brittany for good. If clearing my name means bringing James down—"

"It's too risky. I don't want you involved."

She swiveled in his arms to confront him. "I make my own decisions."

He held her closer, and his dark eyes glimmered in the starlight. "Stubbornness can get you killed. Let me drive you to Orlando, away from all this."

She shook her head. "I remembered David's floor safe. I may think of something else that's helpful.

"You're in danger here."

She snuggled contentedly against him. "I trust you to keep me safe."

His sharp intake of breath whistled through his teeth, and when he spoke, his words were quiet, tortured. "Jenny trusted me, too."

Frowning at the pain in his voice, she cradled the rough stubble of his cheeks in her hands. She suspected Jenny's death was the source of the pain he so often tried to hide with his slow, easy grin and teasing words. "Would talking about her help?"

He stood so quickly she had to catch herself from toppling onto the deck. She followed him to the opposite side of the deck, not knowing which drove her more—her own curiosity or her desire to help him exorcise his personal demons.

With his back to her, he gazed across the gulf. Expecting him to twist away, she placed her hand in the center of his warm, bare back. He didn't move.

"You never speak of her. Don't you trust me?"

"Trust has to work both ways." He leaned briefly against the pressure of her hand before stepping away. "If I tell you about Jenny, you'll never trust me again, and I don't think I could live with that."

"It can't be that bad."

He turned toward her, his face a mystery of angles and shadows in the starlight. "I don't want to lose you, Angel."

Despite her joy at his admission, she recognized the underlying horror in his voice, and her elation plummeted with a quickness that made her giddy.

He clutched her fiercely against his chest and buried his face in her hair. Wrapping her arms around his waist, she laid her cheek against his thundering heart. "Nothing you say can turn me away from you."

His bitter, tortured laughter echoed across the dark, calm water. "You give me too much credit."

"And you sell yourself short."

He released her and drew back, his face grim with resignation, but his gaze never left her face. "You'll find out sooner or later. It was in all the papers a year ago. I'm surprised you don't already know."

A year ago she'd been preoccupied with breaking free from David and forging a new life for herself and Brittany. News events in those days had washed over her like white noise. "If it's bad, I'd rather hear it from you."

He laughed again with a rancorous chuckle that ended like a sob. "It's bad all right. Bad enough that I tried to drown myself in the bottom of a bottle for months afterward."

She tensed, holding her breath, prepared for the

worst, but doubting his revelations could be as ap-
palling as he'd hinted.

He dropped his gaze and grew suddenly still. As
if in sympathy, the breeze died, and the lap of waves
against the hull ceased. The only sound was the rasp
of his breathing.

"You think Frank and Sidney are responsible for
Jenny's death," he said.

"That's what they told David."

He shook his head, slowly, deliberately. "Carleton
James's paid killers didn't shoot Jenny."

She jerked her head up in surprise. "Who did?"

When he met her gaze, his eyes reflected the agony
of a man who had stumbled into hell and couldn't
find his way out.

"I killed her," he said.

Chapter Eleven

"I don't understand." Angel had lost her memory, but temporary amnesia hadn't hampered her ability to gauge people. He had confessed to a crime, but Jordan Trouble wasn't a murderer.

He dropped onto the bench, threw his arms wide and gripped the deck railing with both hands. "From the moment I regained consciousness in the hospital, I've struggled to understand what happened."

"You don't know?"

"I can't remember clearly."

"Didn't the police investigate?"

"Internal Affairs left no stone unturned." He patted the bench beside him. "You'd better sit down. It's a long story, and it started about this time last year."

THE REAL ESTATE fraud file on his desk had ballooned to a thickness of eight inches, but Jordan was no closer to zeroing in on the scam artists than he'd been four months ago at the start of his investigation.

He shoved away from his desk, crossed to the coffeemaker in a corner of the Criminal Investigations Department and was draining the unappealing sludge from the bottom of the pot into his mug when someone tapped him on the shoulder. He whirled, sloshing coffee over the rim of his cup.

"That stuff'll stunt your growth," Jenny Argeroux said.

He grinned at the uniformed patrol officer, whose head didn't quite reach his shoulder, and mopped his hands and cup with a paper towel. "Speaking from experience, short stuff?"

"Another crack like that," she waved a folded newspaper beneath his nose, "and I'll give this to Panowski. When he takes the credit for solving your case, you'll have only yourself to blame."

"Which case?" Jordan grabbed at the paper, but she flitted out of range.

"The real estate scam."

She followed him to his desk. Shoving aside the holstered gun at her hip, she settled into the empty chair beside the cluttered surface of his work area.

He eyed the petite officer with affection and resisted planting a kiss on her freckled nose. "Anyone ever tell you how great you look in uniform?"

She aimed her deep blue gaze at the ceiling. "Oh yeah, clunky shoes, Sam Browne belt and starched trousers are the latest thing in sexy. I have to beat guys off with my truncheon."

He suppressed a grin and shrugged. "You want sexy, you can always ask for an assignment in undercover vice, like nabbing unsuspecting johns. Then you could wear short skirts, high-heeled boots, big hair, push-up bra—''

She smacked him playfully with the newspaper, then flipped it open and spread it across the chaos on his desk. She poked at one section with her finger. ''Be serious and take a look. I picked this up when my shift ended, and the ad jumped out at me.''

A quarter-page advertisement in big, bold type for a new development east of town caught his eye. Jenny was definitely on to something.

''It's the same language, same MO as the first one.'' He couldn't keep the excitement from his voice.

The trail had gone cold on the first real estate scam. By the time the Sunset Bay police had received complaints about a bogus company that was selling homes for huge down payments, then splitting with the money, the crooks had folded their operation and disappeared, completely covering their tracks. Jordan had ferreted out a few leads, including a possible connection to local real estate mogul David Swinburn, but nothing concrete had panned out.

''There's a phone number to call for an appointment,'' Jenny pointed out, cocking an eyebrow at him. She had been a patrol officer only two years, and she was already bucking for detective.

He smiled at her enthusiasm. ''I'll make an appointment and get Maggie to pose as my wife. If we wear wires, we can tape their sales pitch, plus we'll both get a good look at the salesman.''

''With any luck, he's got a mug shot in the files.''

"Thanks, Jen." He tousled her cropped sandy hair. "Did you see Maggie when you came in?"

"She just left. Said she caught a murder-suicide at one of the retirement complexes near the golf course and was headed there to start the investigation."

"That'll tie her up for days." He raked his fingers through his hair in frustration. "And Tracy's on vacation for another week."

Jenny's impish grin wrinkled her freckled nose. "You could try putting Rick Panowski in drag and take him to the appointment. Let *him* play your wife."

Jordan laughed. Panowski's runaway ambition to make lieutenant and his willingness to do anything to further his career were legendary, even among the uniforms.

Jenny's expression sobered. "Or you could take *me* with you."

"No way."

"Aw, Jordy, it's not dangerous—or complicated. I just act like a lovestruck bride anxious to own her first home. How hard can that be?"

"With your flair for the dramatic, not hard, but the answer's still no."

She slugged him lightly on his right bicep. "Lighten up! You're pulling your protective act again. I hate when you do that."

"Don't try your feminine wiles on me, short stuff. What part of *no* don't you comprehend?" He felt responsible for her. After all, he was one of the main reasons she'd chosen a law enforcement career.

She narrowed her eyes and lifted her chin. "I'm a trained officer, and I can take care of myself. If you wait till Maggie's free or Tracy's back, you could lose your chance to nail these guys."

"Forget it."

"If you don't say yes, I'll go over your head."

"To the chief?"

"Worse. Your father."

He laughed. "You fight dirty, Argeroux."

"I fight to win."

And, eventually, she did. Her tenacity wore him down. With the chief's blessing, she made up the other half of the undercover team.

At seven-thirty that night, they drove in an unmarked car to the motel where the so-called real estate developer was meeting clients.

Jordan and Jenny activated their hidden recorders and climbed the stairs to the second-floor room. Jordan knocked at the door, standing slightly ajar.

"That you, Mr. Smithfield?" the voice from their phone conversation called out.

"Yes, and my wife, Jenny," Jordan answered.

"Come in and have a seat. I'll be with you in a minute."

Jordan nudged open the door to the dimly lighted suite, and Jenny preceded him inside. At a sudden movement in the shadows, his instincts flashed red alert. He yanked the SIG-Sauer from his shoulder holster, but something punched him in the left shoulder and knocked him off his feet.

"Look out, Jenny!" he cried, just before the nondescript carpeting rose up and smacked him in the face.

"YOU WERE AMBUSHED." Hearing his story, Angel felt more confused than before. "If you were unconscious, you couldn't have shot her."

"She was killed with a bullet from my gun." The neutrality of his voice hid his obvious agony. "The Internal Affairs investigation concluded I had already drawn my weapon, and my hand must have convulsed on the trigger when I was shot. Jenny was standing in front of me when I fired. She died instantly."

Heartsick, Angel placed her hand on his knee. "I'm so sorry."

"God knows, I loved her," he said softly.

"Would you have married her?"

"Married her?" He looked at her as if she'd grown a second head. "Jenny was my kid sister."

A fist in the stomach couldn't have winded Angel more. "Your sister?"

"She went into police work because of me. I was responsible for her. And I killed her."

"You mustn't blame—"

"I should have been more alert, or entered the room first, or—"

"Don't torture yourself with should-haves." Her heart ached for him, and she longed to wrap her arms around him, but the stiffness in his bearing held her off.

"My father blames me, and so does Ted, Jenny's husband. In fact, my whole family has written me off." His voice held no self-pity, no emotion of any kind, just a deadness that turned her blood cold.

"They can't understand—"

"Dad's a retired police chief. He studied the IA report backward and forward. The report exonerates me, but Dad still believes Jenny's death was my fault. And he's right. A good cop always looks out for his partner."

She yearned for some way to ease his suffering. He had shot and killed the kid sister he loved, who'd regarded him as her hero and followed in his footsteps. How could he expect his family to forgive him when he couldn't forgive himself?

"Jenny's death is why you never returned to the department?"

"No cop would feel safe with me as backup. And how could I trust myself?" The bleakness in his face wrenched her heart. "I put away my gun and haven't touched it since. Then I resigned from the force and used my pension money to buy this cabin cruiser."

Oblivion. Exile. Emptiness. Nothing.

She shivered. The name he'd given his boat described his state of mind. She wished she could siphon away his anguish and make him whole again, anything to free him from his all-consuming guilt and soul-crushing sorrow.

A memory of the unopened vodka bottle in the

bulkhead cabinet flashed into her mind. The demons he'd tried to drown now had names. He'd lost too much—his sister, his family, the work he'd loved. How could any man withstand what he'd experienced without cracking under the load?

But Jordan Trouble wasn't just any man. He was inherently kind and capable and generous. He didn't deserve the tragedies life had dumped on him.

Ignoring his rigid posture, she knelt beside him on the bench and drew his head against her heart. He stiffened and tried to pull away, but she held him fast.

"You might as well stop resisting. I can be as stubborn as you."

"I don't want your pity," he said with a low growl laced with misery. Breaking from her embrace, he rose and circled the cabin to the bow. Determined, she dogged his steps.

He braced himself at the rail, a lonely shadow above the dark open water. Leaning against the rail beside him, she placed her hand over his. "What I feel for you isn't pity."

Jordan searched her upturned face for signs of the pity she denied. Her eyes glittered, but not with sympathy. Slowly, the hard, cold shell around his heart shattered like a stone splintering beneath a hammer's blow. His defenses fell away, and unbearable pain flooded him. He'd barely steeled himself against it before the bolstering presence of Angel's love inundated his agony and washed it away.

With a strangled cry, he gathered her in his arms

like a shield against his grief. She loved him in spite of what he'd done, accepted him with all his flaws. God knew, he didn't deserve her. He should send her away before he tainted her further with the misery of his life.

But he needed her. He wanted her. Since Jenny's death, he'd been a dry husk, void of feelings and only going through the motions of living, but Angel had given him a purpose and taught him to experience joy again.

And Carleton James intended to kill her.

Ignoring the tenderness in his heart and the hot, fierce longing pulsing in his groin, he thrust her at arm's length. "Get some sleep. We'll need clear heads tomorrow."

She didn't protest, but her dazed, hurt expression haunted him long after she'd gone below.

MAGGIE HENDERSON DIDN'T BOTHER with greetings or waiting for Jordan and Angel to take a seat in David Swinburn's formal living room the next morning.

"Did you have any idea what was in Swinburn's safety deposit box, Trouble?"

With her barely contained energy, nervous pacing, slender frame and fiery red hair, the petite detective reminded Angel of a stick of dynamite, seconds from detonation.

"Good morning to you, too, Mags," Jordan said with an amused grin. "You remember Sara?"

Maggie stopped pacing and nodded at Angel. "Looks like I owe you an apology, Ms. Swinburn."

Hope fluttered through Angel like a fresh breeze. "You're dropping the murder charge?"

Maggie cocked her head to one side and skewered Angel with a probing glance. "That depends."

"On what?" Jordan asked.

At his tone and his refusal to look at her, desolation washed through Angel. All business in his investigator's role, Jordan seemed even more remote than Brittany, who was over a hundred miles away.

Maggie nodded toward a quartet of chairs in a far corner, away from the windows. "We'd better sit. This gets complicated."

Stifling a longing fueled by memories of Jordan's tender kisses and the reassuring strength of his arms, Angel sank onto an antique chair covered in yellow brocade and concentrated on the assertive detective. "You don't still think I killed David?"

"What I think isn't the point." Maggie hovered on the opposite chair as if ready to leap to her feet in an instant. "What counts is evidence—and right now, all the hard evidence points to you."

Angel's hopes plummeted. More than anything, she wanted the charges against her cleared and James caught, so she and Brittany could resume their life together. Before last night, she would have included Jordan on her want list, but he'd withdrawn behind a cold, impenetrable shield that shut out his pain—and everyone and everything else along with it.

She glanced at the tall, handsome man whose easy

manner once again hid the terrible agony he suffered. Last night, when she'd heard his account of shooting Jenny and how his family had turned their backs on him because of it, her heart had ached for him. He'd made it clear he didn't want her pity. And he hadn't wanted her love. Judging from his subsequent chilly behavior, she gathered all he wanted was to wreak vengeance on Carleton James and his hired assassins and then be rid of everyone, her included.

When he folded himself into the seat next to her, dwarfing the chair with his large frame, his honest male scent of sunshine and salt water made her stomach clutch with desire. She gave herself an inner shake. She had to concentrate on proving her innocence and quit mooning over a man who didn't want her.

"The evidence against Angel—uh, Sara," he was saying to Maggie, "is all circumstantial."

Maggie shrugged. "At this point, it's the best I've got."

Jordan frowned. "What about your case against Carleton James?"

The energetic detective balanced on the edge of her seat. "What case? All I have are the counteraccusations of the woman already charged with Swinburn's murder, some vague notations of monies paid by Swinburn to James—"

"Don't forget," Jordan interrupted, "I clearly heard Frank and Sidney say James instructed them to kill Sara and her daughter."

Maggie quieted suddenly and leaned back in her

chair, her expression communicating a peculiar gentleness. "You've had a rough year, Jordy. You won't make the most credible of witnesses."

He sighed and tunneled his long fingers through his thick hair. Angel felt his pain but held back from going to him and circling him in her arms. After last night, she was certain he would push her away.

"You're telling me—" exasperation colored his voice "—you have *no* case against James?"

"No hard evidence," Maggie agreed. "Not yet."

Angel wrung her hands in frustration. "You found *nothing* in the safety deposit box to incriminate James?"

Like a dynamo powering up, Maggie grew more animated. "Thanks for reminding me. I wouldn't call a million and a half bucks nothing."

Angel gasped, and Jordan's jaw dropped.

"A million and a half?" he said. "Cash?"

Excitement thrummed through Angel like an electric current. "*That's* the money James is after."

Jordan scowled. "Profits from his phony real estate deals."

"Probably, but I can't connect the money to James," Maggie said. "We've got zip to correlate him to the scams and nothing but Sara's word to tie him to Swinburn's homicide."

The detective's gaze met Jordan's and Angel saw a flash of understanding arc between the two cops.

"So set a trap with the money," Jordan suggested.

"It might work if Sara contacts James, tells him

she has the money and will give it to him if he promises to leave her and Brittany alone.''

''He won't let me live,'' Angel said with a shiver. ''I'm a witness to David's murder.''

Maggie nodded. ''But James doesn't know you don't trust him. You'd wear a wire, ask leading questions. Since he intends to kill you anyway, he may tell you everything—which we'd then have on tape.''

''No way.'' Jordan's voice was hard, unyielding.

Maggie looked puzzled. ''You don't think James will talk?''

''He'll talk, but there's no way you're putting her in that kind of danger.''

Maggie hopped to her feet and balled her hands on her hips. ''What kind of cop do you take me for? We'd have the meeting place surrounded. James wouldn't have a chance to look cross-eyed at Sara before officers'd be all over him like ants on a picnic.''

Heat flushed Angel's face. ''Quit talking about me as if I'm not here. I make my own decisions, and I'm willing to take the risk.''

Jordan's eyes burned black with anger. ''Aren't you both forgetting something?''

Angel glanced at Maggie, then mirrored her shrug.

He rammed his hands in the pockets of his jeans and slumped in the chair. ''You have a mole in your department, Mags. With someone feeding info to James, how can you be sure he'd show up? And if he does, how're the cops going to keep Angel safe if you don't know which one of your guys is on James's payroll?''

Angel blinked in amazement at the stream of profanity that sprang from Maggie's delicate lips. The detective finished her tirade and confronted Jordan. ''So now what?''

''You'll need a totally different plan.'' He arched an eyebrow, watching for Maggie's response.

She shook her head. ''Just a variation.''

He looked skeptical, but Angel, anxious to end her ordeal and reunite with her daughter, would grasp at any straw.

''*I'm* willing to hear it.'' She shot a warning glance at Jordan, daring him to intervene.

He rolled his eyes toward the elaborately sculpted plasterwork of the ceiling but said nothing.

Maggie flicked a wary glance his way before focusing on Angel. ''I know one cop I'd trust with my life. I'll have him guard you from James.''

''Who?'' Angel asked.

''Jordan Trouble.''

Jordan exploded from his chair like a shuttle on liftoff. ''You're out of your mind!''

Maggie folded her arms across her chest, tipped her chin and faced him down. ''Am I? You're the best cop I know, and the only one I can guarantee *isn't* on James's payroll.''

He locked his jaw tight, and Angel spotted a vein in his neck, ticking like a time bomb. Turning his back on the women, he strode toward a window and stared out across the pool as if forgetting they were there.

When he finally spoke, his quiet words were ragged and strained, as if ripped from his heart. "I couldn't keep my own sister safe. I'm not about to have anyone else depending on me."

Maggie studied him for a moment, then shrugged. "It's your call. If you come up with a better plan, let me know. If not, Sara goes to trial for Swinburn's murder."

He didn't respond, and the detective turned to Angel. "If I could think of another way..."

Angel nodded. "Thanks."

When Maggie left, Angel crossed the room to Jordan, who continued to gaze out the window. She slid her arms around his waist, laid her cheek against the taut muscles of his back and felt him stiffen beneath her touch.

"Don't." He ground the word out through clenched teeth.

Anger mixed with caring, almost choking her. He couldn't allow one mistake, no matter how monumental, to ruin the rest of his life. From the little he'd told her of Jenny, his sister would have hated the way he was punishing himself over her death.

"Don't what?" Frustration fueled her temper and loosened her tongue. "Don't love you?"

He sighed. "Don't—"

"Don't try to clear my name so I can have my daughter back? Don't ask you to take responsibility for anything but wallowing in your grief?"

Breaking free of her embrace, he whirled to face her, his face dark with fury. He opened his mouth as if to speak, then clamped his jaw shut.

His size and power, combined with his fury, should have daunted her, but she was too angry, too desperate to notice. "*You* don't want to get involved, fine. Just jump on your boat and sail off into the sunset. I don't need your help."

She spun on her heel toward the exit, but he caught her arm.

"Where are you going?"

She jerked free. "What difference does it make?"

He flinched as if she'd struck him, and his shoulders sagged as the anger left him. "I care what happens to you."

"Those are only words," she shot back. "I'm going after Maggie. Between the two of us, we'll come up with a plan to force a confession out of James and prove my innocence."

He closed his hands over her shoulders and forced her to meet his gaze. "Can't you understand? It's *because* I care about you that I can't be responsible. You need someone emotionally uninvolved, someone you can count on—"

"If not for you, Frank and Sidney would have killed me days ago."

With a tortured moan, he pulled her against his chest and buried his face in her hair. Locking her arms around him, she reveled in the warm security of his embrace until, abruptly, he released her. The harsh set of his face made her last hope falter. With unbearable sadness, she caressed the strong line of his jaw.

She would have turned to leave, but he grasped her hand and pressed it to his lips. His kiss burned her palm, but she couldn't pull away.

His expression remained determined, but his eyes warmed as his gaze met hers. "If we hurry, we can catch Maggie."

"Catch—" Surprise shook her. "You mean—"

"If we're going to lure James here, we have a lot of planning to do."

Chapter Twelve

Talk about a lose-lose situation, Jordan thought gloomily. And he'd plunged into it with his eyes wide open. If he'd refused to go along with Angel and Maggie's scheme, the women had been prepared to tackle James alone. Helping them, however, wasn't necessarily doing them a favor.

Nobody knew, least of all Jordan, how he'd react in a crisis—whether his training would automatically kick in or his memories of shooting Jenny would paralyze him, rendering him worse than useless.

As if his doubts weren't enough, the whole setup was wrong. He could feel it in his gut. Just because things had gone smoothly until now didn't mean catastrophe wouldn't strike at any moment.

During Angel's telephone call, offering to meet and return the money, James had asked for time to consider her proposal. Jordan had figured James needed an opportunity to contact his spy in the P.D. to check for a trap. An hour later, when Angel called James back as requested, he agreed to meet her at sundown at the Swinburn mansion.

An hour before Carleton James's scheduled appearance, Maggie arrived at the estate, bringing a trunkload of electronic paraphernalia.

Jordan surveyed the equipment and scratched his head. "How'd you smuggle this stuff out without explaining to anyone at the station what's going down?"

Maggie grinned as she untangled wires. "I stuffed it in two duffel bags marked athletic equipment and told them I was starting an all-girl soccer league."

"The chief'll skin you alive when he finds out," Jordan warned.

"Before or after he gives me a commendation for solving Swinburn's murder and the real estate scams? Now, take off your shirt."

He had avoided looking at Angel as he stripped. Every time he caught sight of those big brown eyes, filled with trust and affection beneath her wispy bangs of soft brown hair, he wanted only to hold her, to promise he wouldn't let anything happen to her. He'd have a hell of a time convincing her, however, when he hadn't convinced himself.

Assuming an air of cold detachment, he'd allowed Maggie to wire him for two-way communication, then turned away while she attached the mike and transceiver to Angel's smooth skin. While Angel shrugged back into her blouse and tucked the trailing antenna into the leg of her jeans, he kept his gaze on the sketch she'd drawn of the estate grounds and reviewed their plan.

Just before sundown, Maggie would switch on the

recording equipment in her car, out of sight in the garage, then hide inside the rear gates until James's vehicle had passed through. After he entered the house, she would slip into the hallway outside the study. Meanwhile, Jordan would wait in the study bathroom, poised to rush to Angel's assistance at the first sign of difficulty.

Once Maggie had James's incriminating statements on tape, she'd signal for backup on her police radio, then she and Jordan would grab James in the study, and Maggie would make the arrest.

Piece of cake.

Then why was he pouring sweat as he waited for Angel to bring James into the study? Despite the frigid air streaming from the ceiling ducts in the bathroom, a thin trickle of perspiration ran down Jordan's spine and pooled at his waist, where a holster held the .357 Magnum Maggie had supplied him.

He hadn't wanted to accept the revolver—he never wanted to hold a gun again—but he'd be a fool to face James, and possibly Frank and Sidney, unarmed.

"I'm approaching the front door." Angel's words, spoken softly into the mike hidden in her bra, carried through Jordan's earpiece. "This is it."

He didn't hear the door open, but he caught Angel's gasp of surprise."

"Treat or treat." Sidney's familiar voice rolled through Jordan's receiver.

"Good evening, Ms. Swinburn," Frank said. "I believe you have a package for us?"

"Maggie..." Jordan's pulse thundered in his head

as he whispered into his mike to the detective, "Where's James? What the hell's happening?"

"James was driving and the only one in the car when it pulled through the gates," she answered. "I don't know where those two came from—or where James went. I'm calling for backup now."

Jordan waited while she communicated her request over her radio.

"Where are you, Maggie?" he asked.

"Slipping in the back door."

"Just keep moving, Ms. Swinburn." Frank's voice reverberated in Jordan's ear. "We don't want any trouble."

"Neither do I." Angel's voice was cool and steady. "But that's an awfully big gun you have pointed at me and it's making me nervous."

Good girl, alerting us that he's armed.

Jordan wished he was half as calm as Angel sounded. Rage shook him as he pictured James's hired assassins with Angel in their sights. Part of him wanted to jerk his gun from its holster and rush the bastards, bullets blazing. A cooler, more rational side realized Angel would be in the line of fire. Drawing his weapon could be fatal to the woman he loved.

Déjà vu.

"I don't want any trouble," Angel said reasonably.

Jordan heard the door open as she entered the study, and her voice sounded not only in his earpiece but through the bathroom door, as well.

"I want to return to Mr. James what rightfully belongs to him," she said. "Where is he?"

"He's around," Frank said, "waiting for his money."

"Easy, Angel," Jordan whispered into the mike at his collar. "Maneuver them in front of the desk, just as we planned to do with James."

"If you'll have a seat," Angel said, "I'll get the money."

"I got a better idea," Sidney said. "*You* sit down and tell me where the money is."

"Fine," she said. "I'll just sit behind the desk—"

"Keep your hands where I can see them," Frank ordered.

"Of course." Jordan heard the squeak of Swinburn's desk chair as she sat.

"Good girl, Angel. Maggie..." Jordan barely breathed the name into his mike. "Are you in position?"

"I'm in the hall outside the study. The door's closed. Looks like James has flown the coop."

"Let's do it, then," Jordan said. "Everyone ready, on my signal."

"Yes," Angel spoke aloud, "I'm ready, uh, to tell you where the money is."

"Now," Jordan whispered into his mike and threw open the bathroom door.

At the same instant, Maggie, gun drawn, rushed in from the hallway, and Angel lunged beneath the heavy mahogany desk.

Jordan flung himself across the room, landing on

Frank before the gunman could fire, toppling him backward in his chair and pinning him to the floor. Frank's pistol skated across the carpet toward Maggie, who pressed her weapon against the thick folds of Sidney's neck.

Wrestling Frank to his feet, Jordan wrenched the gunman's arms behind his back and clamped on the cuffs Maggie tossed him. Angel skittered from beneath the desk, retrieved Frank's automatic from the floor, removed Sidney's from his jacket and handed both weapons to Jordan.

Tucking the guns in the waist of his jeans, he noted her face had gone pale, except for slashes of high color on her cheeks. Her brown eyes blazed like molten honey.

The whole operation had gone seamlessly, smoothly. No shots fired, no one injured. But the danger wasn't over.

He jerked Frank's arm. "Where's James?"

The handcuffed man shrugged. "Last time I saw him was when we crawled out of the trunk of his car."

"His car!" Angel said. "He'll get away."

"I don't think so." Maggie grinned and lifted a ring of car keys from her pocket. "He'll have a long walk."

Jordan heard the wail of approaching sirens. "And a police cordon to cross." He nudged Frank's shoulder. "Get moving. You guys are going for a ride."

Maggie ushered Frank and Sidney into the hall toward the front door and met Panowski coming in.

"You folks okay?" he asked.

Jordan tugged Frank's and Sidney's weapons from his belt and handed them to Panowski. "Yeah, Rick. Everything's under control."

The detectives left with their prisoners, and Jordan looped his arm over Angel's shoulder. "Ever thought about going into police work? You seem to have a knack for it."

"I couldn't take it." She laughed and shook her head, ruffling her short brown hair. "Too much excitement."

They walked toward the rear courtyard, crowded now with police cruisers, flashing lights and uniformed officers. She stopped suddenly and lifted her face toward his. "It isn't over, is it?"

"It?" A sinking sensation hit his stomach. With Frank and Sidney caught, Angel no longer needed his protection. She and Brittany could return to their apartment and their lives. And he could take off for Key West and oblivion again. The prospect brought him no pleasure.

"They haven't caught James," she reminded him.

"They will. It's just a matter of time."

BUT CARLETON JAMES ELUDED the police dragnet. By the time detectives secured a warrant to search his house, James—and his oceangoing yacht—had disappeared.

"Where do you think he went?" Angel asked Jordan as they boarded *Heavenly Days* in the thin light of dawn.

Jordan headed for the galley. "International waters. Once he's twelve miles offshore, United States' authorities can't touch him."

"And after that?"

She settled on the galley bench. Weary as she was after a night at the Sunset Bay police station, she still enjoyed watching Jordan make coffee. She would never tire of gazing at his broad, muscled shoulders, thick, sun-bleached hair and slow, easy grin.

"He'll probably head for the Caymans." Jordan dumped water in the reservoir and turned on the coffeemaker. "Even if all his laundered money isn't stashed in a Cayman Island bank, he can access it from there."

An inexplicable shiver shook her, and she glanced around uneasily. "What if he isn't on his yacht? What if he's hanging around here?"

Jordan sat next to her and pulled her into his arms. "Not a chance. The police combed the entire neighborhood. Maggie herself directed Panowski's search of my boat."

She snuggled into the reassuring warmth of his embrace. "Then why do I feel so jittery?"

"Fatigue." His fingers brushed her hair from her forehead and traced the line of her cheek, causing a different and not unpleasant restlessness. "And delayed reaction. You went through a traumatic experience last night."

She shook her head. "Working with you and Maggie made it seem like child's play."

He grunted in disagreement. "You were in danger

from the get-go. What if Frank had shot you first, *then* looked for the money?"

The familiar pain haunted his eyes, and she caressed the strong line of his cheek, wishing for some way to erase his heartache. "But he didn't."

Jordan tightened his arms around her. "We were all lucky. Frank Maricosso and Sidney Stepman have rap sheets longer than my arm—and that doesn't include the contract murders we can't pin on them. Those guys are cold-blooded killers who'd as soon shoot you as look at you."

"What's going to happen to them?"

"They're turning State's evidence and testifying against James."

"So much for honor among thieves."

Jordan grimaced. "They're looking out for their own skins. In return for implicating James, they're hoping the state attorney will reduce their sentences."

"Reduce?" She bolted upright in his arms. "How can the attorney do that? Those men are too dangerous to be walking the streets."

"Frank and Sidney won't be freed. They're bargaining for life in prison instead of death sentences. And speaking of jail, what happened with you while Mags and I were in interviews?"

"I called Michael from the station. After checking with Maggie, he contacted Judge Zacharias. All charges against me have been dropped." Her spirits soared in spite of her fatigue. "I can bring Brittany home now."

"You should get some sleep first."

"I can't. Not now."

She wanted him to be happy for her, but his expression had turned gloomy. She'd expected having her name cleared to change everything, but proving her innocence hadn't brought back Jenny—or Jordan's faith in himself. Even though he held her, he seemed a million miles away.

"You'll need a car to drive to Orlando," he said.

"That's a problem. Maggie said mine's been impounded as evidence."

He released her and crossed the galley to pour coffee into mugs. "I'm heading back to Sunset Bay Marina. If you want to ride along, you can borrow my car until yours is released. If you call the Erskines now, they can bring Brittany to meet you at the marina."

No *us,* only *you.*

He'd withdrawn, shut her out, and no matter how much she loved him, she couldn't penetrate the wall that protected him from the horrible pain he suffered from killing his sister.

He handed her coffee and sat across from her.

"I care for you more than any woman I've ever known," he said, as if he'd read her mind, "and because I care, I'm getting out of your life." His eyes were dark with an agony she could only guess at.

"But—"

"I have to sort things out, come to terms with the fact I killed my sister before I can get on with my life. I've made some progress, but I have a ways to go."

"I could help."

He shook his head. "This is something I have to work out for myself, and I have no idea how long it could take—a year? Ten? I can't ask you to put your life on hold while I get my head on straight."

She wanted to argue, demand that he let her stay, but the stubborn, unyielding look in his eyes convinced her she'd be wasting breath. She'd already learned that once he'd made up his mind, it would take the equivalent of an atomic blast to shift him.

"Who knows," he said with a shrug and his slow, easy grin, "someday years from now, I may show up on your doorstep."

Although her heart was breaking, she returned his smile. "Who knows?" she echoed, wanting to cry.

He pushed to his feet. "Now that's settled, how about some breakfast?"

She shook her head. Being near the man she loved while he pushed her away had become torture. "The sooner we head back to the marina, the better."

His grin faded, and after a grim nod, he left her and went on deck to disconnect the lines. Carrying her coffee and fighting tears, she followed and climbed after him to the flying bridge.

He appeared nonchalant, but the tension in his jaw and the bleak look in his eyes conveyed how difficult his decision had been. She would have continued her argument to remain with him, but she doubted her staying would bring him any happiness, not until he'd exorcised the ghosts and demons that haunted him. And he obviously didn't want a witness to his struggle to overcome them.

He turned the key at the controls, the powerful engines rumbled to life, and he steered the boat toward the channel.

"We'll head into the Gulf," he yelled above the noise of the motors. "It's longer that way, but faster."

She nodded, gripped her coffee mug and hoped the wind would dry the tears from her cheeks. In a couple of hours, she would walk out of his life for good. He had saved her from hired killers and a possible death sentence, but after today, she'd probably never see him again.

Her heart ached for him and the solitary, tortured days that stretched ahead of him. She faced loneliness and unhappiness, too, but she would have Brittany. Jordan, whose family had ostracized him when he needed them most, would have no one.

They cruised deeper into the Gulf. She watched the land dwindle and disappear over the horizon and wondered how what should have been one of the happiest days of her life had turned so miserable. Conversation was impossible above the noise, so she curled into a chair and consoled herself with thoughts of Brittany.

Despite her earlier refusal to sleep, the hum of the huge engines and the motion of the boat lulled her, her eyelids drooped and she drifted into uneasy dreams.

Sudden silence jerked her into awareness. The engines had stopped, and she wondered if they'd reached the marina. Stretching, she opened her eyes.

The boat rocked alone in an endless expanse of water, and a slender, middle-aged man with thinning hair, watery blue eyes and wrinkled clothes propped himself against the rail.

He held a gun at Jordan's temple.

At her movement, the intruder glanced at her without lowering his weapon, and his thin face cracked in an evil smile. "So, Sleeping Beauty awakes. Allow me to introduce myself, Mrs. Swinburn. I'm Carleton James."

Chapter Thirteen

Angel jerked upright, flicked a glance at Jordan, standing grim-faced beside the wheel, and looked back to the intruder. "How did you get onboard?"

"I've been here since last night, in the bedroom closet."

James's hideous grin made her shudder. "But Maggie had the boat searched—"

"Panowski did the looking," Jordan interrupted with a knowing nod. "I'll bet my pension he's the spy you've had in the department all along."

"Very astute," James said. "Panowski located me in the closet. I gave him instructions for the captain of my yacht to meet me today, twelve miles due west of Sunset Bay."

"And we're supposed to provide your ride to the rendezvous?" Angel said.

"You'll be in no condition to provide anything except food for the fishes," James stated coldly.

"Why kill us?" Jordan asked.

She marveled at his coolness, when James's threatening expression and the small cannon he held terrified her.

"Your cover's blown," Jordan continued, "you're on your way out of the country, your money must be stashed in offshore banks. What good will our deaths do?"

"I'm a tidy man. I don't like loose ends."

"At least let Angel go. She's done nothing to harm you."

She loved Jordan more at that moment than she'd ever loved anyone. She had to live, for Brittany's sake, but she couldn't bear the thought of life without Jordan. Better a life lived hundreds of miles apart than one without him. "We'll take you to your yacht," she said. "There's no need to kill us."

"Ah, but there is. My name isn't really Carleton James. I've had dozens of names. And as long as I can make money in this country, I won't be exiled to some foreign hole where I can't enjoy what money I have. In a few months, I'll reappear somewhere else, Texas, perhaps, with a new name, new face and fresh prospects."

"And you'll bilk hundreds more innocent people out of their hard-earned cash," Jordan said with a scowl.

James sighed impatiently. "It's what I do. Just like you're a policeman, and you, Mrs. Swinburn, are a parent."

"How many more families will you ruin before you're through?" Jordan demanded hotly. "How can you sleep at night?"

James laughed with a high-pitched effete giggle. "Better than you. I, at least, didn't kill my own sister."

Angel's temper snapped. "You would have, if there'd been money in it."

"I'm not a total scoundrel," James said easily.

She ignored the warning shake of Jordan's head. "You'll have a hard time proving it."

"And, please, don't bore us with your contributions to charities," Jordan said sarcastically. "Giving away other people's money doesn't qualify you for sainthood."

As he spoke, Jordan kept his eye on James's gun, except for a brief moment, when he lifted his gaze to Angel and flashed a silent message she couldn't interpret.

"I'm not all bad," James said, "or else I wouldn't offer to tell the real story of how your sister died."

Jordan's face paled beneath his tan. "The *real* story?"

Angel froze in her seat, holding her breath and waiting for James's explanation.

James, pointing the gun with one hand, studied the manicure of his other. "You can go to your watery grave a happy man, Trouble, knowing that you didn't shoot your sister."

Jordan sank into a chair beside her as if his knees had given way. "I didn't?"

James edged away, creating a safer distance between him and Jordan. "When Frank shot you, Sidney grabbed your sister. We assumed you were already dead, so Frank handed me your gun.''

If she hadn't been watching closely, she might have missed the rage that flitted briefly over Jordan's face before his features settled into an expression of relief. ''*I* didn't kill Jenny?''

''No, although that's what I wanted the police to think. I, Lieutenant Trouble, am your sister's killer. It was an easy matter to shoot her, then replace the gun in your hand.''

''I didn't kill her,'' Jordan muttered in stunned disbelief.

''I shot her, and now I intend to shoot you. If there is a heaven, as the ridiculous name of this vessel implies, you will soon be having a family reunion there.''

''Wait,'' Jordan begged.

Despite her terror, Jordan's strange reaction puzzled her. He licked his lips nervously, his hands trembled, and he appeared on the verge of tears.

''If you're not all bad, like you say,'' Jordan said with an unfamiliar whine, ''you'll grant a man one last request?''

''That depends on the request,'' James said.

''A drink,'' Jordan pleaded, and the trembling in his hands expanded throughout his body. ''I need a drink. A man shouldn't have to die stone-cold sober.''

Angel's emotions ricocheted between terror and confusion. This quivering beggar was a Jordan she'd never seen. No wonder he wanted her out of his life.

He was ashamed for her to witness his degradation when he lost his fight against his demons. He hated her pity.

"Angel should have a drink, too," he said. "A big one."

James rubbed his chin. "A bon voyage toast? Why not? In this wretched heat, I wouldn't mind a drink myself."

"All I have is vodka," Jordan said. "It's in the galley."

"You first." James waved toward the ladder with his gun. "I'll bring Mrs. Swinburn."

Jordan rose unsteadily to his feet and started down the ladder. Angel descended next, followed by James, who kept her covered with his huge gun the entire time. Jordan stumbled into the lounge, and Angel and James followed.

"The bottle's over here." Jordan crossed to the cabinet that separated the lounge from the kitchen. "It's never been opened—I was saving it for a special occasion."

"You only die once," James quipped. "Now, no sudden moves or you'll die *without* that drink."

She turned her face away, unable to witness Jordan's surrender to the tremors of alcoholism another instant, wishing he could die like a man. This quivering wreck before her wasn't the Jordan she knew. She glanced back at him as comprehension dawned. His behavior had to be an act. But what could he hope to gain with his charade? And what chance did he have with James's gun on him. The glint in the man's eye told her he wouldn't hesitate to shoot at the least suspicious movement.

She issued up a last, silent prayer, thankful Brittany was with the Erskines, who loved her and would care for her once her mother was dead.

Jordan saw Angel avert her face, but he couldn't allow the distaste in her expression to distract him. He needed that bottle. Moving slowly as James had ordered, he swung open the cabinet door. "See, a whole bottle of Absolut, and the seal's not even broken."

His hands shook with fear. He was doing something he'd promised himself he'd never do again. Resigned, he knelt and reached into the cabinet. With an awkward lurch, he knocked the vodka bottle over.

"Good thing the top's on tight," he muttered, loud enough for James to hear.

Reaching deeper into the cabinet, he passed over the bottle and tightened his fingers around the object that had been his goal from the start, his backup gun hidden in the recess. Deftly, he slipped it from its holster and flicked the safety.

"I've got it," he said. "Drinks for everybody now."

"About damn time," James complained.

In one smooth fluid movement, Jordan straightened, aimed and fired. In the same instant, Angel screamed, and James's gun roared as he fell to the deck.

An ominous silence filled the lounge.

"You okay?" he asked.

James's wild shot had obliterated the sliding glass door behind her. In shock, she stared at Jordan, wide-eyed, and nodded. He knelt beside James, removed the gun clenched in his fist and felt for a pulse.

"He's dead."

Angel nodded again.

He had to get her out of there before she went to pieces. He jammed his gun and James's in his belt, grabbed Angel with one hand and the bottle of Absolut with the other, then pulled her onto the deck and up the ladder to the flying bridge.

He settled Angel into a chair and reached for his ship-to-shore radio. "Operator, patch me through to the Sunset Bay Police Department."

After a brief explanation to Maggie Henderson, he turned to Angel. "Maggie's having Panowski arrested, then she's boarding the police boat to meet us here."

Like a sleepwalker, Angel nodded numbly.

"It's okay," he assured her. "It's all over now."

She lifted her gaze to his, and her eyes held a thousand questions.

With a jolt, he realized he still gripped the bottle of vodka. He raised it to her in salute and watched a shock of dismay cross her face before he pitched the bottle high into the air. It spiraled in the sunlight in an end-over-end arc before plummeting into the shining deep water off the starboard bow.

"You never wanted a drink at all, did you?"

He shook his head. "It really is all over now. Once

Maggie's finished her investigation, we can go to Orlando and bring Brittany home.''

"We?" Her face brightened, but her tone was tentative.

"We. You, Brittany and me. No ghosts, no demons.''

With a happy cry, she leapt from her chair into his arms. "I love you, Jordan.''

He crushed his mouth to hers, then twirled her in his embrace. When he broke free to breathe, he cradled her face in his hands. "Looks like I'm going to be drunk on love the rest of my life.''

With her hands clasped behind his neck, she flung back her head and studied him. "You're all right? You're sure?''

"I'm sure. I love you, Angel—my Angel.''

Epilogue

The sign at the streetside entrance to Mary Tiger's read Closed to Public for Private Party. Jordan, trim and fit in his custom-tailored tuxedo, climbed from the car and offered Angel a hand.

Stepping out of the limo into the cool breeze and October sunshine, she surveyed the packed parking lot. "Looks like an overflow crowd."

"You know cops. Promise 'em free food and drink and they show up in droves." His smile crinkled the tanned skin around his midnight-blue eyes, free now of guilt and pain. "Have I told you how fantastic you look?"

"Once or twice," she teased, arranging the full-length skirt of her ivory-satin gown with one hand as she tucked the other through the crook of his arm. "Shall we run the gauntlet?"

Together they marched into the palm-thatched *chickee*. Her vision took a moment to adjust to the dimmer light of the room after the brilliant sunshine. When she could see clearly, her eyes filled with happy tears at so many familiar and welcoming faces.

From behind the bar, Mary Tiger greeted them with a wide grin and her usual sarcasm. "Took you long enough. Thought you were gonna skip the reception and go straight to the honeymoon."

"Now, *there's* an idea," Jordan called back.

"Yeah," the bartender cracked, "and if you'd arrived much later, every cop in the place would be drunk and disorderly."

All members of the Sunset Bay Police Department not on duty filled the room. At a table near the door, Hal Walden rose to his feet and lifted his glass. "You've gone and done it now, Angel. Didn't your mama warn you about marrying trouble?"

"That's *borrowing* trouble," Jordan corrected good-naturedly, "and I'm one cop that can't be borrowed or bought."

The others laughed at the puns and crowded around, slapping Jordan on the back, squeezing Angel's hands and mixing good wishes with wedding-night innuendos.

The band, apparently exhausting its repertoire of Jimmy Buffet tunes, segued into a Whitney Houston ballad as Jordan and Angel worked their way through the crowd of relatives and friends toward the head table.

"Mommy!" Brittany, dressed in teal-green satin and white lace tights, wriggled from Henry and Fiona's grasp and darted toward her.

"Hello, short stuff." Jordan intercepted her and swung her into his arms. "You did a great job scattering rose petals at the wedding."

Her chubby face crinkled in a smile. "Hi, Daddy."

Jordan hugged his new daughter even tighter.

His amused gaze met Angel's over Brittany's blond curls. With patience, affection and good-natured teasing, he had created a strong bond with Brittany, and the child had slipped easily into calling him Daddy and thinking of him as her father. And he would always think of her as his own.

Brittany beamed with pleasure. "Pwetty, Mommy."

Jordan set her on her feet. "You and your mother are the prettiest ladies here."

"Maggie, too," Brittany insisted.

Angel glanced at Maggie, dressed in the same teal satin as Brittany, who had stood as her maid of honor. She was sitting at the head table with her head bent toward Michael Winslow, laughing at something the attorney had said.

"Mind if I steal your daughter?" a deep voice behind Angel asked.

"Hello, Dad." Jordan enveloped the older man in a bear hug. "Thanks for serving as my best man."

Angel's heart swelled with gratitude. After Carleton James died and the facts about Jenny's death and Panowski's treachery had been revealed, Jordan, his father and Jenny's husband, Ted, had reconciled. They were a family again.

Breaking from his son's embrace, Matthew Trouble cleared his throat and swiped at his eyes with a big fist. "Don't know about this 'best man' label. That should belong to the groom. Now, mind if I take Brittany with me? How about it, young lady? Ready for some lunch?"

Brittany placed her small hand eagerly in his. "Gwanpa Twouble, want cake."

"After your mommy and daddy cut it," Matthew promised, and clasped Angel's hand with his free one. "Welcome to the family. It's good to have a daughter again. And a granddaughter." His eyes clouded with tears. "She reminds me of another little girl I used to know."

"Who?" Brittany asked.

"A little girl named Jenny." Matthew and Jordan exchanged glances, and Angel knew they both were missing Jenny Argeroux, that they would always miss her, but that her death would never again come between the father and son.

Angel stretched on tiptoe to kiss Matthew's weathered cheek. "Thank you for making us part of your family, Papa Matt."

"Police families stick together," he said, "and now that Jordan's a detective again—"

A brassy fanfare from the band interrupted him.

"Ladies and gentleman," the leader said, "may I present the bride and groom."

Jordan opened his arms, and Angel slid into them to the applause of the guests. But after a few seconds, everyone but Jordan faded into the background as, drifting with the waltz, she basked in the glow of his love and reveled in the rightness of his embrace.

"This is the most perfect day of my life," he said.

Head back, she locked her gaze with his. "Mine, too. I only wish your Jenny could be here."

"She is," he said, releasing her hand long enough to tap his heart.

Angel nodded, thinking of her parents and the memories of them she carried. If she hadn't been so vulnerable after their death in a traffic accident, she would never have married a man like David Swinburn. They would have approved of Jordan.

Other couples joined them on the dance floor, including Brittany, dancing with her stocking feet on top of Papa Matt's black patent shoes as he held her hands to balance her.

Angel nodded toward them and enjoyed Jordan's smile as he caught a glimpse of the mismatched pair.

"We'll name our next little girl Jenny," she promised him.

"What about our son?"

She leaned back and taunted him with a teasing grin. "We'll name him after his father, of course."

"Of course," he said warily, obviously aware of the mischief in her eyes.

"We'll call him Trouble," she said with a laugh.

Jordan stopped still and considered her with raised eyebrows and a devilish smile. "Angel, baby, you already have more Trouble than you can handle."

Before she could reply, he closed his lips on hers, and his embrace lifted her off the floor. Laughter, applause and the strains of music disappeared beneath the heat of his lips.

When he finally broke the kiss, she gasped for air.

"If this is the kind of Trouble you mean," she promised breathlessly, "I'll take all I can get."

They were both laughing when he kissed her again.

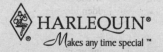

HARLEQUIN®

I N T R I G U E®

COMING NEXT MONTH

#517 HER BABY, HIS SECRET by Gayle Wilson
Men of Mystery

Previously thought dead, ex-CIA agent Griff Cabot reemerges to save his baby daughter from kidnappers. But the ransom demanded is an assassination. Can Griff get to his child in time—and forgive the only woman he's ever loved for not telling him he was a father?

#518 UNDERCOVER FIANCÉ by Sheryl Lynn
Elk River, Colorado

Daniel Tucker is the only man for the job, an expert determined to flush out Janine Duke's deranged pursuer—and hell-bent on shaking her up in the process. Posing as her overly demonstrative "fiancé," Daniel seems to be taking his role all too seriously. Leaving Janine to wonder if she's in more danger of losing her heart to Daniel than her life to a madman....

#519 THE STRONG, SILENT TYPE by Jule McBride

Years ago, moments before her wedding, Claire Buchanon's bridesmaid was killed and her fiancé Dylan Nolan disappeared and became a suspect. Now, Claire's about to marry another man when a mysterious stranger begins to stalk her. But he is hit by a car and left with no knowledge of who he is. Claire finds his eyes eerily familiar... Is it Dylan—and what is he doing back in her life?

#520 SECRET LOVER by Shawna Delacorte

There's nothing more alluring than a mysterious stranger with sinfully sexy lips. Mystery writer Andrea Sinclair found herself inexplicably drawn to Jim Richards—mind and body. It was like she already knew him. But Jim, who was instantly attracted to Andi the woman, needed to keep away from Andi the investigator, the only person alive who could expose his carefully hidden identity.

Look us up on-line at: http://www.romance.net